There Something About Paris

A Novel

By Vivien Lacey

Text Copyright © 2018 Vivien Lacey
Front Cover Illustration © Emma-Louise Smith

All Rights Reserved

ISBN-13: 978-1723023712

Dedication

For my family,

With Love

Acknowledgements

*To my friends Victoria and Emma-Louise,
for your invaluable support*

Chapter One

Xavier led Sienna along the dimly-lit misty back streets of the Latin Quarter on the Left Bank of Paris. They walked down a narrow, cobbled and eerily quiet alley. The almost-full moon seemed to look down on them curiously as they negotiated the wet mottled cobblestones which glistened with traces of sparkling ice, a reminder of the snowfall the day before.

"Here we are! Voici la Boîte de Jazz!" ("Here is the Jazz Club") Xavier said, heaving a sigh of relief as it was bitterly cold by now and the street was shrouded in a haunting darkness, but for an old-fashioned street lamp which looked as though it had been there forever and watched over a century of passers-by. Xavier knocked on the thick, worn wooden door, which had traces still of the layers of paint which had covered it during its life. A figure that one could hardly make out opened the door, but in the dark entrance Sienna could only decipher the form of an old-ish man, clothed from head to toe in what appeared to be washed-out denim of some kind.

"Salut!" He nodded to Xavier, "Entrez! Entrez!"

The unimpressive entrance led straight into a long, rectangular and rather smoky semi-lit room which had a lingering fragrance of musty tobacco. Sienna tottered across the flagstone floor, polished by centuries of footsteps, wondering why on earth she'd bothered to wear her highest stilettos. They usually made her feel quite elegant and more confident, but tonight they just made her feel a tad awkward. The deep, earthy and moody strains of a saxophone reached her ears as she drank in the seductive ambiance of the room. They navigated the room slowly, dodging between couples sitting on aged velvet sofas and chaise-longues, a lot of which were seriously in need of re-upholstering. There was a haze of smoke in the air from those who puffed on their *Gauloises*. Here and there people lounged alone on the easy chairs whose worn velvet had seen better days. Many sported stains where someone at some stage had spilt some unidentifiable drink. They had the air of having been bought at an auction. These chairs definitely weren't in their prime. In the coppery light of the room, Sienna again drank in the atmosphere. She felt the haunting yet wonderful music entering into every cell of her body; it was exquisite. Suddenly she knew why Paris was going to be special. Some people were dancing, some together but mostly twisting and turning on their own, sensuously and dramatically and always in time to the music.

Sienna had always loved Jazz, but never experienced anything quite like this. She'd never quite understood modern Jazz. This, however, was different. It was traditional and reminded her of New Orleans and the blues of the Deep South. She sat down next to Xavier on a dusky pink sofa, whose large wooden buttons were badly scratched, but were a nod to its previous existence. Xavier was already deep in conversation and gesticulating madly, as the French do, talking quickly in incomprehensible French to an interesting-looking man with deep-set eyes. He puffed on a long pipe with an air of insouciance. Sienna sipped the large glass of Pernod she had acquired from a ridiculously handsome waiter with shiny black hair and large almond-shaped eyes. He spoke some English in an impossibly French accent. *The kind*, Sienna thought, *that had likely turned many a maiden weak at the knees over the years…*

At the front, in the corner near to the sax player, Sienna observed a gentleman in a grey striped gilet, worn over a loose burnt-orange cotton shirt, with cuffs turned back casually. Interestingly, she noted a large burn on one of his arms. His stone-coloured cords were tucked into ageing, crinkly leather boots that tapped rhythmically in time with the music. He bent forward to retrieve a *Gauloise* from an old, well-worn parchment-like bag and, as he did so, she saw that he was not young. He did not have the air of a man who sat on a park bench watching the world go by – he was more like someone who sat at an easel and used his imagination to make images. He reminded Sienna of a character from her book of Jack Vettriano's paintings. He had a certain loucheness and a *je ne sais quoi* coupled with a look that said, "I don't give a damn". *Intriguing, yet questionable...* she thought. As Sienna and Xavier got up and wandered past him to the bar area, he raised an eyebrow in Sienna's direction and embraced Xavier warmly; Xavier introduced him as "Alphonse". A voice softly called Alphonse to attention and made him turn around.

"Lily!" he gasped, "*Comme tu es mignonne ce soir!*" ("How cute you look this evening!")

Lily was alluringly slender. She wasn't ostensibly beautiful. Her dark, soulful eyes sat dreamily above high-sculpted cheekbones. Her porcelain skin shone radiantly in the lamp-light. She held herself as though she owned the place, but somehow not in an arrogant manner. Here was a woman who knew her worth. As Lily bent over to kiss Alphonse on the cheek, Sienna admired her lithe body which was clad in a figure-hugging dress with dark, shiny beads the colour of marcasite. Each bead glimmered and shone as she moved, and her dress clung to her body as though it was just an extension of it. Sienna was near enough to notice the air was subtly filled with the aroma of Lily's perfume. It was always "Y" by Yves St Laurent, she later learned – a sophisticated and alluring perfume which suited her personality exactly. Her delicate features and bright red lips made her a paradox to behold. She was a strong woman, yet distinctly feminine with a discernible vulnerability about her. She carried a black cigarette holder with a silver top which she periodically lifted from the ashtray on the small wrought-iron side table beside her. She took a long, rather sensual puff on it leaving behind traces of her deep-red lipstick along its length. She frequently tossed her black fringed bob in a coquettish manner as she talked. At present she was leaning towards Alphonse. *Was he just a friend?* Sienna mused. *Hmm... his mistress probably. It is France.* Xavier had seen her staring at Lily.

"Lily? *C'est un original!*" ("One of a kind!") He shrugged in his Gallic manner.

Well she's definitely not run of the mill, thought Sienna, *but then, is anybody I've met here?*

Sienna's eye moved around the room. People seemed to know each other and wandered effortlessly from person to person or group to group, leaving those who were clearly in the first flush of *amour* to gaze into each other's eyes and nestle up on the chaise-longues. Sienna perused the décor, which had clearly been carefully chosen and displayed, for maximum effect and atmosphere. The crumbling grey brick walls were left undecorated and displayed all kinds of sketches, paintings and posters in different mediums: mainly with a twenties aura, it seemed. Some were rather tarnished but fitted in with the surreal theme of things. Thinking about the twenties, Sienna suddenly realised that Lily's beaded dress and sleek black bob seemed very much of that era and that maybe it was a "twenties night" as many others had also adopted the style of dress that was popular then. Carrying her drink, Sienna wandered along the now quite crowded room and looked around at her surroundings, almost in awe. Here and there on the old grey flagstones were large, weather-beaten terracotta pots in burnished hues. Some still had moss or algae growing on them in parts, from their earlier days outside. The pots cradled tall, unusual looking plants of all shades of deep greens and faded browns. There were no flowers – just exquisite foliage. She noticed side tables made from what looked like recycled timber and driftwood which gave the impression of being *objets trouvés* (found items) from various *marchés aux puces* (flea markets).

It was as Sienna sat down on a faded-green, slightly ripped velvet chair that she observed another "character". She later discovered this was Theodore (Theo). He was neither young nor old in appearance but oozed the vibrancy of a much younger person. Dressed very casually and individually, he tapped a sandaled foot that poked out of his grey denim dungarees, in time to the music, as he sat on a wooden stool. He had spotted Alphonse.

"*Sacré bleu! Alphonse, mon vieux!*" he called over to him. Sienna noticed that he had silvery-white hair, tied back in a ponytail with a thin rope band and was sporting a long-ish white beard. Xavier joined them and clearly was acquainted with Theo, but then Xavier seemed to know everybody, by dint of his people-orientated job. He was clearly good with people and had an easy charm.

"*Comment ça va, Xavier?*" ("How are you, Xavier?") The two men embraced and launched into a long, animated conversation which seemed to include the opening of a new first-class restaurant on the Left Bank, the best patisserie in the Marais district, details of Theo's latest wine cellar acquisitions and his recent purchases from the local flea market. *Enchanting!* thought Sienna, feeling fortunate to be shown around by Xavier, who was always bursting with pride to show off "his" city and their way of life.

Sienna knew very little about Xavier, except that he was very likeable and made her laugh a lot. He worked for Thomas Cook in Paris and they had been introduced through a friend, before her arrival in Paris, as someone who would show her around and charged a reasonable fee to boot. It certainly helped that he spoke fluent English, though Sienna was anxious with others to speak as much French as possible. Her French was good and her accent, by all accounts, did not sound too English, just attractively so. Some even thought she was Belgian! Still, she was studying here for a whole year, so there was plenty of time to become fluent. Sienna was feeling very drawn to the French way of life. She had been over here before as a tourist when young; but this was different. Now she was privy to life beyond the tourist track. Oh, how she longed not to be "a mere tourist" and to be one of them – a Parisienne. Somehow it seemed more interesting than being English.

By now, a striking little lady (who Sienna soon found out was Mireille) was perched on Theo's lap. *Now who's she?* Sienna mused. Mireille was a small, bird-like creature who looked as though she could burst into song any moment with "*Non, Je ne regrette rien*" ("No, I don't regret a thing" by Edith Piaf). Her dark hair and dark, olive skin gave her a distinctly foreign appearance. Although she chatted away in fluent French, Sienna noticed she had a kind of regional accent. Perhaps she was Algerian. Theo introduced his friend to Sienna.

"*Voici Mireille*, Sienna!" ("Here is Mireille!") Sienna shook her hand. *Oh dear*, she thought, *should I have kissed her on the cheek? But then...once or twice?*
Mireille turned out to be a dancer who had been well-known at the *Folies Bergère*. She animatedly complimented Sienna on her French and asked her what she thought of the Jazz. Sienna replied that it was captivating, as was the whole ambiance of the night and the interesting people that filled the room.

"I feel privileged to be here." Sienna smiled. Xavier had disappeared with another group of people chatting at the bar as Lily headed in Sienna's direction.

"Sienna, I'm not working tomorrow. Would you care to join me for lunch?"

"Oh yes!" Sienna enthused, "I only have one early morning lecture tomorrow."

They arranged to meet in Saint-Germain-des-Prés, a well-known area on the Left Bank, which was steeped in history. Sienna knew it was full of art galleries, artist shops, bookshops, cafés and bistros so "just up her street". She looked forward to some girly talk instead of Xavier's lively banter. She loved his company, but she needed to make other friends. Xavier, however, was very informative, easy-going and easy on the eye! This little side-line of his – showing people around the city and introducing them to places tourists didn't know, brought him in some extra income. He seriously needed the money in order to pay for frequent weekend trips, and sometimes holidays, with his long-term girlfriend, Gabrielle. He had met Gabrielle in Paris, but she was now studying in Barcelona and had limited funds to get home, so this had been the answer. They would maybe live together one day, Xavier told her, when she had finished her studies and was able to get a job.

It was soon time to go home and to reflect, dozily, on the evening's happenings. Sienna had had her senses awakened at the *Boîte de Jazz* (Jazz Club) in a way she had never experienced before…and she felt excited. Sleep did not come easily as she thought about all the people she had met and could still hear the strains of the saxophone echoing in her head, but she felt peaceful and ready for her new chapter. Her nerves at meeting new people in Paris seemed to be disappearing, although tomorrow might tell a different story.

Chapter Two

Sienna awoke and looked out over the wet, glistening rooftops where a cold mist was gently lifting, and the distant buzz of early traffic was just beginning to awaken the bustle of the Parisian day. She yawned and wandered sleepily towards the small kitchen which housed a kind of hotchpotch of cupboards. Fitted kitchens didn't seem as popular in France as they were at home. The cupboards held just a few jars and packets of essential food items. The fridge contained a few eggs, some slightly mouldy-looking Camembert, half a bottle of leftover wine (which Xavier would laugh at – he always said, "Whatever *is* left-over wine, Sienna?") as well as a few yoghurt pots which could well have been out of date by now. *Hmm…time for a shop!* Sienna thought, as she sipped on a steaming bowl of hot chocolate and munched on a single croissant which was sadly not exactly fresh. She seemed to be surrounded by interesting food shops here in the Latin Quarter. There were patisseries, *boucheries*, etc., and bistros galore. She smiled as she remembered the night before. She could already see light at the end of the tunnel of trepidation and aching homesickness that came over her out of the blue. She knew it would take time. Friends of the family who had spent years as ex-pats had warned her that it had taken a long time to settle, and, after all, she'd only been in Paris a month and a half! Stretched out on the sofa she settled into the deep abdominal breathing she had learned at her yoga classes in England; it usually worked to calm her down. She didn't feel up to the exercises, though. It had been a big leap of faith to quit the familiarity of England, her friends at university, her supportive family always at the end of the phone. Still, she could speak to them! She'd felt a huge need to break away though and find the direction she should be heading in. She rebuked herself for not feeling overwhelmingly grateful to her parents. They had been so generous in paying for the rent of the basic, but cosy, studio apartment in the 6th arrondissement of

Paris. She was living on Rue de la Chaumière, an area steeped in artistic tradition – even the likes of Gaugin had been at the Academy there, deep in the heart of the Latin Quarter and a great spot to live. Xavier was showing her around, at her parents' expense; though he didn't charge much. *But he's your only friend…*whispered a little voice inside her head, though it was counteracted quickly by another louder one which cheerfully said *Ah, but you've met us now!* as she pictured the faces from the night before at the little Jazz Club. So many interesting people to look up again…

Sienna remembered, as she shook off her sleepiness, that she was, in fact, going to meet Lily at lunchtime. There was, sadly, an essay on Stendhal to be finished, though she decided to leave it until the evening when her concentration for more serious issues might be more intact.

Sienna wandered along the beautiful tree-lined avenues of the nearby Jardin du Luxembourg, where groups of young children were happily playing on swings and laughing and tumbling from slides. In other areas the landscape was breath-taking and there were so many statues; the French liked their statues. She sat down on an empty bench and took in her surroundings. The last of the season's sun shone kindly on her face and the fresh air was invigorating. The rest of her walk would hopefully finish the process of clearing away the cobwebs from her mind.

In Saint Germain, the cobbled streets were again a reminder of the history and character of the area. Outside the Métro entrance Sienna stopped to give a coin to a beggar who stared hungrily at her with wide, hopeless eyes. The whites of his eyes were bloodshot, and he had a creased and wrinkly countenance that was etched with the wear and tear of life outdoors. It moved her almost to tears; beggars always had this effect on her. She looked at his mangy little dog, who also had bloodshot eyes, nestling beside him on a frayed and dirty blanket. *And I think I have problems!* She rebuked herself again.

She had agreed to meet Lily outside an antique shop on the nearby Rue Jacob. It was cold, and the sky looked that kind of heavy mid-grey colour that made her think snow might be on the way. A slight, svelte figure in navy blue appeared, seemingly from nowhere, and almost bounded around the corner tugging along a rather impish little dog, who was constantly pulling at his lead.

"Now settle down Fifi," she said. "It's not time to play!" She spotted Sienna and gave her a kiss on each flushed cheek, followed by a hug that had little power behind it, possibly because of her delicate frame.

"Fifi, sit!" Lily bent down to chide her little dog, an interesting poodle mix. Sienna had observed that Paris was full of Fifi's and Fido's. The French adored their dogs, along with their statues. Lily looked incredibly chic, in her long navy wool coat with matching leather boots and electric-blue legwarmers that curled over the top of her boots like crestless waves. She carried a huge aubergine-coloured bag and an electric-blue cashmere scarf was tossed around her neck and knotted in some mysterious way that only French women seemed to know. Lily wore very little make-up except a touch of mascara and a dot of blusher on her flawless but pale skin. Her striking black bob framed her delicate features and made her look stunning in an almost fragile way, just like a piece of delicate porcelain china.

"I thought we'd go to the Café De Flore, Sienna. I know you don't like the tourist track, but you really must go just once. You probably already know that it's famous because Hemmingway and other well-known writers and thinkers used to pass their time drinking and exchanging ideas there, so there's atmosphere and history."

"Oh yes, I've heard about it. I would love to go as I'm still getting to know lots of places that aren't tourist traps with Xavier and I'm beginning to feel like I'm one of you and not a tourist which is the general idea!"

The café stood on a corner, timelessly iconic. Waiters bustled to and fro, carrying all kinds of delicacies and often their famous creamy hot chocolate drink. People took photos of them, of each other and of the food. Sienna enjoyed people watching. Despite it being a tourist attraction, she could pick out the French clientele easily by their appearance, and there were quite a few that looked like interesting characters. She knew that women *of a certain age* were respected, if not revered, in France. At the next small, round table was a striking lady in the autumn of her life. She had white-ish hair, worn to her shoulders which was pushed back off her face with a thin bandana, tied in a knot at the front. She wore huge, white framed sunglasses and just a dash of red lipstick. Her gingham coat was pale blue and white with large buttons and billowing sleeves. She bent over to a tiny dog with a matching gingham waistcoat. There was no way this elegant lady wasn't French! Sienna admired her elegance and insouciance as a waiter greeted her with a kiss.

"*Bonjour, Madame Leclerc.*" He smiled and gave her the menu and a titbit to the dog.

Sienna thought she would be an interesting person to talk to, but, of course, her identity would forever be a mystery.

"Sienna, you're day dreaming! What would you like to eat? This is my treat for you. To re-welcome you to our Jazz Club, our circle of friends, and of course to Paris…"

Sienna ordered eggs with herbs and smoked salmon, which were excellent, and a Kir Chablis. Lily had a Quiche Lorraine washed down with a fine white *Mâcon* wine. Sienna looked around at the Art Deco décor which seemed to give the place a soul. The atmosphere was priceless, quite unlike the menu tariff which was not for the fainthearted! She wanted to know more about Lily, who was by now sitting smoking elegantly as she sipped coffee. Fifi was asleep, curled up under an elaborate wrought-iron table and looking peaceful. Lily told Sienna that she had been born in the Marais district where, in fact, she still lived. Her mother had been a dressmaker and well-known in Paris for her sewing and meticulous attention to detail. Her father was a baker who owned a very popular *boulangerie*. As a child, Lily remembered them as always busy, her mother with her clientele and her father getting up at the crack of dawn to make fresh croissants and baguettes for the day. He also made speciality breads of which he was very proud. His *boulangerie* was well-known for its artisan bread. People came a long way to taste his *pain au noix* which contained nuts and *pain au lardons*, which contained bacon. There were so many breads available that people walked in and often got a trifle confused!

"*Et là qu'est-ce que c'est, Monsieur Bouffon?*" ("And over there, what's that one, Monsieur Bouffon?") could be heard frequently by excited customers. Sienna couldn't imagine getting excited in her bakers at home! The tourists from overseas would often ask for a "*pain au chocolat, s'il vous plait!*" and were surprised to see it was actually a chocolate croissant and not bread at all. Sienna listened eagerly to the story.

"Oh, I'd love to meet your parents, Lily! Are they still in the Marais?" Lily lowered her eyes and paused as though not eager to respond.

"They died, Sienna. A few years back now in an accident." She clearly did not want to give details, so Sienna, saying how sorry she was, asked no further.

"Yes, and I used to help in the shop at weekends with my brother. When *Papa et Maman* died my brother and I moved in with *Grand-mère*. I was old enough to work then. She was elderly and very strict, so I really wanted a place of my own. I decided to become a seamstress like my mother. My brother always wanted to paint but, through lack of money, he had to go to work in a garage. I worked hard but, as I have a keen eye for fashion, I was delighted to eventually be offered a place working for *Vogue* magazine, where I helped style the models and did alterations on some exquisite designer clothes."

Lily had worked for Chanel, Dior and Yves St Laurent. One day a very dashing gentleman called Hervé arrived on the scene. He wore an immaculately cut suit (probably Yves St Laurent) with shiny pointed leather shoes and carried a black cane with a gilt knob. He was not young and looked very aristocratic. She had never met anyone that carried a cane. Spotting Lily on her knees, pinning and tacking one of Yves St Laurent's creations on a willowy model, he approached her gently and asked her name. "Lily," She had replied, shyly. He asked if she would stand up and clearly liked what he saw. Lily had, even then, a shock of striking black hair, framing her exquisite features and a slender figure on her tall frame. Lily looked excited as she recounted how he'd asked her to attend his studio and thought she would make a splendid model.

"The rest is history," she laughed "I became a very well-known model and even appeared on the cover of *Vogue* – but that was then. I still model now, but they mainly look for new and younger talent."

"Wow, Lily! I'm not really surprised though. You are so elegant. What a lovely story. Before you finish, could I just ask you about Alphonse?"

"Now, now!" Lily laughed. "Later! I'm hoarse from talking. Let me get the bill and let's explore a bit more of the Latin Quarter together. After all, this is going to be your home for almost a year!" She paid the bill. "*Viens*, Sienna!" Lily put her hand gently on Sienna's shoulder and guided her back through the cobbled streets. It hadn't snowed after all, but there was a distinct chill in the air. Wrapped up in their scarves and both wearing warm gloves, the two girls laughed and chatted as they turned off into a little side-street, Sienna really enjoying Lily's company and knowing they would now be firm friends.

"Where are we going, Lily?"
"Shh! You will see, Sienna."

Chapter Three

They moved along the streets of the Latin Quarter, intrigued by the little boutiques and very old, interesting-looking shops along the way, although it was a much quieter place than Saint-Germain-des-Prés. The first shop appeared to be a shop that sold artists' materials. Even before she peered into the window, Sienna noted the very old exterior with its peeling, dark-mint green paint, weathered door and sills and generally uncared-for look, and yet its appeal was obvious. It fitted beautifully into its surroundings with the old, well-trodden cobblestones and grey-looking apartments and houses, clearly built many years previously. They looked into the window, curiously, and Sienna was amazed. It didn't even remotely resemble anything she'd seen at home. Being interested in painting and occasionally finding the time to draw and paint herself, she usually sought out the art shops when she visited a new place in England. She hadn't done much painting for such a long time though…it was nice to be reminded of it all. The window here was a work of art in itself. Palettes, easels, inks, charcoal, tubes of paint, brushes, pencils, etc., seemed to be placed in wooden boxes which were arranged in defining groups and displayed in front of large canvases, with beautiful abstract paintings done by the medium displayed in front of it. Stunning! A gentleman with a beard and a ponytail was bending to retrieve something from the window. To Sienna's great surprise, she recognised him as Theo from the Jazz Club. He was wearing his dungarees – *surely not the same pair?*

"Oh Lily! Let's go in – please!"

"Lily!" Theo exclaimed as they went in and they kissed each other on the cheek.

"*Quest-ce que tu fais ici?*" ("What are you doing here?") Recognising Sienna, he added, "*Et Sienna! Quelle surprise!*"

The shop did not surprise after the window display. Everything was beautifully grouped and displayed on the old wooden shelves, which were occasionally splattered with paint. On the light-grey dappled plaster of the walls hung exquisite ink and watercolour paintings, which were stunning and atmospheric. Some were painted just in a sepia hue, others had been drawn with coloured inks into intriguing abstract shapes.

"Come and look at my paints!" Theo invited, enthusiastically. "Do you paint, Sienna?"

She nodded. "I haven't done much for years though, Theo…"

Walking around the shop, she gravitated towards the beautiful boxes of watercolours, graded according to colour, in their solid, wooden, compartmented boxes.

"You will not find such watercolours easily in England of this quality, Sienna. If you do, they will be enormously expensive. These were formulated years ago using honey – yes, honey! – and are called *Aquarelle Sennelier*. The textures and colours are second to none – in fact, they were used by several of the great masters."

Sienna fingered them gently and marvelled at the diversity of tones and hues. *The price*, she thought, *was rather like the paints…surreal*. However, she vowed that one day, when she had more money, she would return for these. They stayed a while, making small talk with Theo, then bade him farewell.

"*Au revoir!*" beamed Theo, tossing his ponytail, as a dog would wag its tail. *I still don't have a clue how he knows Lily*, mused Sienna, *but he's so likeable and he's an original, like Alphonse*. Lily could see that Sienna looked a little tired by now.

"Just one more shop, Sienna! The rest can wait for another time, eh?"

Next door was an old bookshop, with weathered, green shutters. There was a display of what were clearly antique volumes in the tiny bay window. How Sienna loved old shutters. They'd had some at home for a while – but a house really needed to be in France to look at its best with shutters, she had decided. They stepped inside a dimly-lit room which displayed row after row of dusty-looking tomes, often with well-thumbed or yellowing pages which sometimes curled at the corners, relaying their age. Many were found in dark, worn, brown leather covers. They stood proudly on gnarled wooden shelves, which were etched here and there with the cracks and notches of time. On the other side of the room there were some grey-coloured, pitted concrete shelves with yet more books. This time they were paperbacks with the marks of time and handling. Sienna loved the smell of books. She picked one up and perused the yellowing pages.

"Ah, Lily!" exclaimed Sienna. "This is *Madame Bovary*, by Flaubert – a firm favourite of mine. I already have a copy in French at home which I've read a thousand times, as I could relate to the character! Looks as though someone else enjoyed it too..." The owner, a short, rotund gentleman wearing a mustard-coloured waistcoat with buttons straining to meet, greeted them. He stood up and Sienna saw a rather red-faced man, who looked as though he enjoyed a cognac or two and *un bon vin* (a good wine). He sported a large handlebar moustache and had twinkly eyes. He introduced himself as Monsieur Dubois and proceeded to chat to Lily at such a pace that Sienna could only pick up the intonation and the waving of his arms. *Gesticulation is a national pastime*, she noted. He sat down again eventually, squeezing his form between a cane chair and his large, antique desk. A small, scruffy black dog of unidentifiable breed lay underneath, nestling on a frayed, wool tartan blanket, staring quizzically with one eye open.

"*Au revoir!*" he called as they left, and carried on feeding the dog, who had a small sign beside him aimed at tourists: "Please do not feed the dog chocolate!"
Sienna skipped along happily, with Lily walking elegantly beside her. Fifi walked slowly by now, ready for her basket and sleep. Sienna kissed Lily and thanked her for a wonderful day.

"Amazing!" Lily said. "Well, I'm off now for a meal with Alphonse…"

"Alphonse, eh?" Sienna teased her slightly.

"Oh Sienna, don't be ridiculous!" She laughed. "You didn't know? Alphonse is my brother!"

Chapter Four

There seemed to be quite a lot of boring essays to catch up on and some important lectures to attend. Xavier had gone to see his girlfriend Gabrielle for a couple of weeks. He was tired and deserved a break, but Sienna would miss him. After two or three days Sienna was developing cabin fever! She'd definitely had enough of her own company and the four walls, so she decided to set off on her own to explore more of Saint-Germain-des-Prés, which was so intriguing and interesting. Before leaving she phoned Xavier, who got in touch with an old friend called Freya. She offered to meet up with Sienna at a well-known café. So, after a brisk walk in the crisp and cold weather, Sienna found herself at Les Deux Magots, only a stone's throw away from the café where she had recently met Lily. Les Deux Magots was similar to the one where she had met Lily in that it was famous as a meeting place for the intellectual and literary elite in Paris, in the days of Hemmingway, Scott Fitzgerald, etc. It was now a tourist attraction and not cheap. To begin with, Sienna found herself feeling a bit disappointed to be going to another tourist attraction; however, Xavier reassured her that the Parisians actually used it too and it was worth a visit!

Sienna sat down and surveyed the menu. *Hmm, croques monsieur, croissants, quiches, foie gras...* She imagined the likes of Hemmingway and maybe Jean-Paul Sartre blending into the atmosphere and scribbling their erudite thoughts over a bottle or so of the very best *vin rouge*. There would have been plenty of artists around too. *Am I falling for the clichés?* she wondered but continued to enjoy her reverie. She espied the lady she was due to meet, easily recognisable from Xavier's description.

"Freya?" She asked.

"Sienna! I am so pleased to meet you!" Freya said excitedly, kissing her cheek.

She had replied in perfect English, which was a welcome respite for Sienna. Freya explained she had travelled far and wide and English was a favourite language. They sat down and ordered a creamy hot chocolate drink; the best Sienna had ever tasted. A rather bohemian-looking lady with an intense manner and pretty face looked at her curiously. Deflecting the attention away from herself, Sienna ventured:

"Tell me about yourself, Freya. Somehow I think you've led an interesting life?" Freya smiled and began to tell how she'd lived in Paris all her life. Her mother had told her there was gypsy blood in the family and she knew it to be true. She was a spirited lady who suffered from wanderlust and had an irresistible impulse to travel here, there and everywhere she felt led to go. On her travels, she'd gathered a collection of bohemian friends and had quite a few in Paris too. Sienna found out later from Lily that she was known for her kind nature and she could often be seen with an assortment of rather grubby, but happy-looking children trailing behind her and dressed in what were clearly assorted finds from the markets and *brocantes* (second-hand shops). Who they were and where they came from was a little nebulous but, having no children of her own, Freya loved to care for the under-privileged and the orphans of the city. She had very little money herself and lived in a one-bedroom apartment.

"Oh…where's that?" Sienna asked with interest. She learned that Freya rented her apartment from a man she knew in Saint-Germain-des-Prés who had a shop below. She shared the shop space with him to sell her interesting finds. Freya loved nothing better than to explore the flea markets and *brocantes* for unusual objects and knick-knacks that others would have thrown away. She saw beauty in old things, retro-style bits and pieces and bric-a-brac. Everything she bought (for a song) seemed to have chips, cracks and marks on them (as Sienna saw later), yet they were full of character. Freya disliked brand-new items, which she described as "soulless". Her furnishings and other pieces that she sold had a timeless quality and echoed the clothes she wore too. Bohemian was her style. Her long ash-blonde, tousled hair hung in make-believe ringlets which she styled with rags as her mother had taught her. She wore a frayed, muted floral band around her forehead, beneath which dwelt her large, expressive eyes. One look into these eyes betrayed her deep, emotional self and the spirituality which was so important to her. Freya only wore long flowing dresses or gypsy-style skirts and cotton blouses that occasionally looked as though they had seen better days, but – somehow – she pulled it off. Quite often she wore flat, unusual sandals, but when it was cold, as it was then, she donned her favourite weathered leather boots which she had picked up from a shop in Brittany which was closing down. Her whole demeanour belied her age of almost forty. Freya "thought young", acted the same and still maintained a youthful innocence about her, despite a string of failed relationships and a sometimes rather lonely existence.

"Well Sienna – that's a lot about me! What about you? Xavier tells me you are here studying the language, but that you are keen to see the real Paris rather than just the tourist spots, like the Eiffel Tower?"

"Oh, I'm having a wonderful time doing that," Sienna replied. "How do you know Xavier, though?"
Freya replied that she'd known Xavier a while and that they met up quite often at a little Jazz Club in the area. "Have you been?" she asked.

"I've been, and I really enjoyed the night," replied Sienna, thinking it was nice to express her thoughts in English for a change.

"I'm going there with Ernst next week," said Freya. "Do come along and you can meet him too. It's *Gypsy Jazz* night, which I love with a passion." Sienna asked her who Ernst was.

"Ah, he's the chap I mentioned earlier who owns the shop I sell from and my flat. A very good friend of mine – you'll like him."
Freya had secretly hoped that Xavier would be there. Although not at all like her more eccentric friends and quite a bit younger, she was intrigued by Xavier's charm,

his easy manner with people and his dark, brooding good looks.

"Oh, he's gone to Barcelona to see his girlfriend…" replied Sienna when Freya had asked if he'd be there.

"Ah yes, Gabrielle," Freya said quietly. "*Tant pis.*" ("Too bad.") She knew that he had a girlfriend, but she could still hope, couldn't she? She then asked if Sienna would like a light lunch at her abode, after which she would take her somewhere else special if time allowed. The two girls walked arm in arm along the cobbles like long-lost friends. Sienna felt a close affinity to the quirky Freya already. She loved her spirited attitude, her freshness of approach to so many things and she found her individuality edgy and intriguing. It wasn't long before they reached the small shop, where Freya sold her wares from. It nestled in a narrow side street of Saint Germain.

"*Entrez! Entrez!*" ("Come in! Come in!") Freya insisted. "*Voici Ernst. Ernst – voilà ma camarade, Sienna!*" ("Ernst, here is my friend Sienna!")

Ernst was a dashing young man with piercing blue, soulful eyes, deep set in a face with a chiselled bone structure that displayed high cheekbones too. He had a shock of dark hair which hung slightly to one side rather seductively over his handsome face. There was a sadness about him which Sienna couldn't quite put her finger on, but she found him very attractive. He was attractive in an unassuming way. He spoke softly as though to have a gentle disposition. The hint of sadness was in his eyes.

"*Entrez, Sienna!*" He held out his hand and Sienna shook it heartily. "*Enchanté Mademoiselle!*" They left Ernst downstairs in the shop and Freya led the way up the spiral staircase at one side of the shop to her tiny apartment on the third floor, part of which was the attic. Sienna was not prepared for what she saw. There was a bathroom, bedroom and attic living room. Knowing that Freya had very little money and that her flat was small, she did not expect what met her eyes. The apartment was tastefully arranged. Freya had lovingly decorated it in a style that was truly hers. Rustic, but different. The ceilings were slanted and painted with chalk paint in a powdery grey, between exposed oak beams. A stripped pine floor ran the length of a fairly long, but narrow, room with a grey linen-covered sofa which was still plump-looking although it had clearly seen better days. This was piled with all sorts of cushions in striped fabrics of varying shapes and sizes and widths which sat alongside old French grain sacks, which were filled and used for cushions too. These were often plain and straw-coloured and sometimes had a muted thin red stripe or two at each end. An old chest of drawers sat in one corner, the drawers of which had been painted in various Provençal colours, giving them an abstract design on the plain wood; they looked stunning. On top sat all sorts of bits and bobs that looked quite expensive, but clearly were not. Several small piles of books were scattered around the room and an old, tall and tarnished grandfather clock stood in one corner, watching over the comings and goings, possibly for centuries in other homes. There were crumbling walls left undecorated and others with paint peeling off them. Earthy terracotta pots were gathered together of all shapes and sizes and placed on rather worn but still vibrant deep-piled Turkish rugs. Everything blended together in collective harmony.

Sienna longed for her new home to look like this, or similar. Freya clearly had an amazing, creative aptitude. The walls displayed all kinds of ink and watercolour paintings, in differing sizes but cleverly grouped. Some of the frames were of dark wood and others of metal. Freya took Sienna into her small bedroom which had an iron bed with bright checked sheets reminding Sienna of the décor of Provence again. A guitar was propped up again an old armoire which undoubtedly held all of Freya's boho clothing and trinkets. The rustic ambiance was completed with a wooden floor covered with several large, thick, patterned rugs. Soft tones and subdued shades blended well together, from the beautiful old ceramics to the large decorative vases. Sienna almost begged Freya to help her re-decorate her flat.

"Of course, *Chérie*!" Freya laughed, "but all in good time, eh? Maybe when winter has gone. *On va manger, oui?*' ("We will eat, yes?") They sat down in the living room to a light but tasty lunch of baguettes, cheeses, olives with grapes and a glass of red wine. As Sienna was leaving, Freya offered to pick her up with Ernst to go to the *Gypsy Jazz* session. Xavier might still be away, so it was a welcome offer.

"Ernst and I will come at eight in his little red car," she said. Sienna drifted off to sleep quite early that night to the strains of Sidney Bechet playing the sax, to the tune of "*Petite Fleur*"– a firm favourite of hers.

Chapter Five

Sienna decided to stay at home for a couple of days to unwind. She was well behind with her studies, as usual. It wasn't procrastination – it was just that she was too busy learning the art of being a Parisienne. Meeting interesting people and exploring interesting places that weren't always on the tourist track stimulated her mind and senses. She became aware of a lot of things she had been missing. Sinking into an old cane chair with a wonderfully squidgy cushion after stoking the log burner in the corner, she looked around with a critical eye at her surroundings. She disliked living in someone else's idea of making the flat a home. The bland-looking walls, in a shade that resembled the magnolia her parents had at home, and rather unexciting curtains looked ready for a change. They were both displaying soft but uninteresting tones and textures. The carpet was worn (but not in a stylish way, as some "aged" carpets are). There were no pictures or paintings – no atmosphere or *joie de vivre*. A solitary bilingual parrot who talked far too much sat in its black wire cage, sulkily. She had agreed to look after him. Sienna wanted to change so much but, as interior design was not her forte, she wasn't sure where to begin. There wasn't a lot of spare time to ponder it all, either. There was so much literature to be analysed and other deadlines with her studies too. She wished she hadn't listened to her father and had gone to art school instead. Since she was a small child she had often sat sketching in the fields outside, watching the farm labourers in the fields and drawing all kinds of interesting people as they went about their daily lives. She studied their demeanour and posture and turned them into character studies on paper. Sometimes she would set up her easel, grab her palette and paints and just paint, abstractly, and from pure imagination. At other times it would be a landscape, maybe in pen and ink and washed over with delicate transparent watercolours. She was aware, though, that she needed to refine her technique as she was totally self-taught. She made a mental note that someday, when money allowed, she would go back to Theo's shop and buy some Dr Martin's inks – the very finest.

At school, Sienna was a very apt and keen student, especially at spoken French. She loved France and the French people, so it hadn't seemed so crazy at the time to take a French degree. When she reached university, however, she found a lot of the literary analysis hard-going. *Oh no*, she thought, picking up a book by Stendhal. *Not another one to analyse until the cows come home...* She had already studied Camus and Proust, but they were next going to foray into Medieval French, which interested her as much as white-water rafting along the Colorado river.

"Crikey!" she moaned, out loud, "Just get me out of this, somebody!"

"*Merde!*" said the bilingual parrot in agreement. It was the year meant to be spent improving her French studies, but it turned into a voyage of self-discovery and a growing passion for all things French and especially of Paris; the city of her dreams. Dreams? Sienna knew she had "arrived", as it were, when the previous night she had actually dreamed in French! She still sat brooding for a while, but then remembered that she had read somewhere "If you don't like your inner voice, get a new one!" It was time for a bit of positivity. Getting up, she put fresh sheets on the bed and lit a single scented aromatic candle. She looked around again at her surroundings. She needed to get some paintings, some unusual architectural house plants and fresh flowers. That would be a start. A bit of *joie de vivre* in her home would help her mood. Looking in the mirror as she passed, a rather tired, pallid face stared back at her. She'd even acquired a spot on her cheek above her cherished dimple. *Disaster! It's* Gypsy Jazz *night in a couple of days and I'm a dishevelled mess.* Sienna vowed to soon call on Lily to help sort out her appearance.

Chapter Six

It was the night of *Gypsy Jazz*. Sienna had given herself a face pack and tied her long-ish brown hair in a circular plait at the back which sat on top of her head, stylishly. She decided to wear some slightly boho clothes for the occasion and pulled out a long, flowing tiered skirt in a muted pattern which she normally wore in summer. She added a navy low-neck blouse with frills at the neck and sleeves, along with lots of wooden bangles of varying hues and textures and a long, silver pendant.

"Yep, that will do! Oh, and my crinkly suede ankle boots with buckles…" She flung a warm, fringed cape around her shoulders as it was bitingly cold outside. It wasn't long before she heard the "toot" of Ernst's car and she ran outside, grabbing her tiny shoulder bag.

"*Bonsoir!*"

"*Bonsoir, Sienna! Ça va?*" Ernst and Freya smiled welcomingly. She got into the little red car and it wasn't long before they arrived at the familiar wooden door. Beaming at the prospect of another lovely evening, Sienna almost ran in, closing the creaking oak door behind her with a hard shove.

Instead of the usual haunting tones of the saxophone, they were greeted by a very different sound – and, therefore, a somewhat different atmosphere – but it was equally appealing and seductive. A young Spanish-looking man was playing guitar in the corner, dressed in what can only be described as traditional gypsy clothing.

"Do you know anything about the tradition of *Gypsy Jazz*?" asked Freya.

"Well, no, not at all!" Sienna discovered it had been started long ago by a chap called Django Reinhardt, who was a gypsy. He invented the *Gypsy Jazz* Clubs. Along with a violinist called Stephane Grappelli, he had begun the "Hot club de France", which was a quintet in the 1930s and 40s.

"So, you see that happened some time ago, Sienna! Today the *Gypsy Jazz* players are called *Manouche Musicians*, as they are *Manouche* gypsies, from where I'm descended – but the tradition has carried on. They play a mixture of guitars, violins and sometimes a bit of clarinet and saxophone."

"Sounds quite a combination."

Sienna was impressed. You could already hear the upbeat guitar music and it was impressive. She looked around for familiar faces. There were several new faces, but soon enough she spotted Lily, doing a rather strange up-tempo dance with Theo, who struggled a bit because of a slight limp. Freya saw her watching.

"Yes, sadly Theo hurt his foot a few years back in an accident, but it doesn't stop him dancing!" With his long ponytail tossing from side to side and his patchwork dungarees, he looked the embodiment of gypsy/bohemian style – *was he a gypsy?* She watched him dancing. Limp or no limp, Sienna got the impression that nothing would ever stop him dancing! Freya decided to dance alone and loved the attention. Her beautifully sculpted frame courted a strappy, fine silk dress which revealed a small but sensual cleavage as she turned and twirled voluptuously in time to the music. Her tiny bejewelled sandals with their small kitten heel picked out the colour of the delicate peonies on her dress. Sienna wondered if she was still single. Despite her apparent former affair with Ernst, Sienna had never heard her mention any other man. Alphonse was in his usual seat, chatting to a few friends that Sienna didn't know; he called her over. She went across and was introduced to a lady called Hélène, who was draped over a slightly tipsy-looking fellow with curly dark hair and large black-rimmed square glasses. Henri was introduced – Sienna thought he looked more intellectual than the rest. He wore a large hand-knitted yellow jumper which gave him the appearance of an under-ripe banana. Hélène, a Peruvian, had a "salt-and-pepper" coloured plait and she was brightly dressed in an orange top and matching skirt with fringes everywhere. Just then, Sienna heard the creak of the heavy front door and turned her head, almost spilling her red wine on a nearby chair. There was Xavier! It had clearly been raining as he cut a rather doleful figure with his dripping hair and drenched stylish mac. He wasn't smiling, and he looked tired.

"Xavier?" Sienna approached him in surprise. "You're not due back until the end of next week. Is everything ok?"

"*Non, pas du tout…*" ("No, not at all…") Xavier murmured. "I'm not stopping – I'm not in the mood. Just one drink, eh?" They moved forward to the bar, past the dancers and the guitarist. Sienna could not help but notice that Freya's dancing had changed. She had now broken into a rather sexy, swirling, voluptuous dance as she cheekily let one of the thin straps of her dress slip down across her arm. Sienna had noticed her glancing across at Xavier. *Ah that's it*, she deduced, *now I know why Freya is alone. She wants Xavier.* Xavier nodded at Freya but then moved straight to the bar, ordered a large cold beer which he downed rapidly.

"What's wrong, Xavier?"

He looked down and spoke in hushed tones. "It's Gabrielle – we're not getting on well at all. Look, Sienna, I need to get back home and have some sleep. Would you have lunch with me tomorrow? We can talk then."

Oh dear, Sienna thought, *that means missing another lecture.*

"Yes," she replied hesitantly. "I would like that." *After all, wasn't Xavier more important than some long-buried French philosopher?* He had become such a special friend. The mood changed somewhat. Xavier disappeared soon after and Freya retired to the bar, where she was later seen looking rather dishevelled and a tad worse for wear…

In the meantime, Ernst came over smiling and asked Sienna if she was enjoying herself. He then told Sienna how beautiful she looked that evening. It reminded Sienna of a very unromantic approach in a club in England when the guy in question approached her with an "Awwwwight? Wanna 'ave a dance then?" Only Ernst had more class! *Hey, this was Paris!* Sienna blushed, not being used to such compliments. She didn't feel particularly beautiful amongst the array of gorgeous Parisiennes.

There was something very engaging and attractive about Ernst's manner. She remembered how, when they first met, she loved his softly spoken yet confident tone. Ernst was equally attracted to Sienna's girlish and somewhat innocent demeanour. He loved the little dimple in her left cheek, which formed as she smiled, and how she tossed her tousled warm brown hair. Tonight, it was styled differently and gave her a touch of sophistication. They stood there, chatting away like old friends. Sienna was, by now, almost fluent so the exchange was easy, and the conversation flowed. It was soon time to go, as they found themselves among the few remaining people there. Before Ernst called Freya over to all bundle into his little car, he leaned over to Sienna.

"Sienna, I really hope to see you again soon?" he said softly in a rather sexy Gallic tone. "I would like that!"

"*Moi aussi*," ("Me too,") replied Sienna, embarrassed by the slight quiver in her voice. She had rarely felt so taken by a man – and so quickly. There had been a student called Nick at university, who was devastatingly good-looking and fun to be with, who had stolen her heart. Sadly, she found him at a party in the clutches of another man, whilst they were still together. After that she had stayed away from men – at least from romantic encounters – but now she was feeling strangely drawn to this rather mysterious French man that she knew so little about. At home, she remembered the spot on her face and her rather worn boots. She critically ran through everything that he might not have liked. Sadly, she did not notice the one thing Ernst was drawn to – and that was her smile.

Chapter Seven

Gabrielle sat in the gloomy silence in the twilight of her little apartment in Barcelona. What was she doing? Where was she going? She felt a sadness mingled with confusion envelope her tiny frame as she huddled up close to the only sources of comfort – a tiny log-burning stove and a tiny cat called Mimi. Xavier had stormed off – she had never seen him "lose his cool" and she didn't know if their relationship was going to survive, or indeed if she wanted it to. How she missed Paris, where she was born. Barcelona was a lively and interesting place, but it wasn't Paris. Her parents had encouraged her to come to Barcelona to study psychology, which she loved. The incredible depths of the human mind, people's interactions with one another, genetic and environmental influences were all things that intrigued her. She was a deep thinker and a sensitive soul. Her parents were well-to-do and had bought her an apartment here, hoping that one day she might sell or rent it out, return to Paris (possibly with a husband) and become an eminent psychologist! Gabrielle, however, although interested in following a career, was much more anxious to marry, settle down and have a family, even if the career failed to take off. As an only child she had missed the companionship of siblings. As she grew up, it seemed her parents were always entertaining or out at the opera with friends. She was no stranger to loneliness and hoped for lots of children to love and spoil. But now Xavier, whom she'd originally thought might be a perfect choice for the father, was possibly not going to be around much longer. She shuddered at the prospect of being alone again. Although Xavier was in Paris, he'd managed to get to Barcelona frequently, if only for the weekend. Now, however, he'd gone and there was only her, the log fire and her small cat, Mimi. Would Xavier ever settle down? She really doubted it.

She loved Xavier and she thought that he loved her. The problems stemmed from his work commitments and his love of travel. In the winter, he was around in his Paris office, but from spring to late summer he undertook quite a few commitments as a courier with his firm, which took him around the world. Clearly, Gabrielle couldn't go too, and she was totally fed up with the situation. It was winter now, yes, but the prospect of another spring and summer loomed ahead. She wanted Xavier to quit his job and find one in Barcelona, where she would be for at least another year. Xavier loved his job. He had wanderlust in his veins and he couldn't see himself settling in one place for long. The problem was he loved Gabrielle too. The rows had become unbearable. Xavier had a short fuse and the sensitive Gabrielle would burst into tears at the slightest provocation. She recalled how they met two years previously. She was at home in Paris and working temporarily in a large Parisian department store, on the Boulevard Haussmann. Gabrielle stood daily, smiling as the elegant ladies passed by her perfume counter and would greet them with a spray of the latest perfume, which often secured a sale. She loved that job and met a lot of interesting and affluent Parisiennes. It wasn't just the chic Parisiennes whom she served, but their boyfriends and husbands (or other people's husbands!) who wanted to surprise the ladies with perfume. One day, a handsome young man hurried towards the counter. He needed a perfume for his mother's birthday. She was an elegant older lady, or as the French say, *Une femme d'un certain âge* (A woman of a certain age) and he wanted a sophisticated perfume. Gabrielle suggested "Femme" by Rochas, with its rich undertones. He quickly paid for a large-ish bottle, which Gabrielle wrapped in delicate pink paper and topped with a large chiffon bow. She could see he was in a hurry – he almost ran away but tripped on an uneven tile and dropped the bottle, which smashed and filled the air with its heady perfume.

"*Zut alors!*" ("Damn then!") cried the young man, who she later learned was called Xavier. Gabrielle summoned her manager and helped clean the mess, explaining that the floor tile was dangerously loose and convinced her manager to replace the perfume. Xavier admired the calm manner in which Gabrielle had dealt with the matter and thought what a beautiful young lady she was, and so asked for her phone number. The rest, as they say, is history.

Mimi the cat padded softly over to her and jumped on her lap. Soft tears fell gently onto her black fur as Gabrielle cried for what could have been. She would ring him tomorrow and tell him they couldn't go on together…

Chapter Eight

Sienna had arranged to meet Xavier the following day for lunch at a small but well-known bistro in the Madeleine district. She took the Métro and arrived on time at the trendy, lively little restaurant, where – despite the cold – people were sitting and talking animatedly outside. *Parfait! (perfect!)* thought Sienna, but she had begun to wonder why Xavier was ridiculously late. She finished her coffee and decided to go over to his flat, as he wasn't answering her calls either. She rang the bell, but it took a while for Xavier to answer. When he eventually did, she was shocked at his dishevelled appearance.

"*Mon Dieu, Xavier! Qu'est-ce qui se passe?*" ("My God, Xavier! What's going on?")

His usually sleek, dark hair was sticking up at all angles, he clearly hadn't shaved and had the bleary look of someone who hadn't slept and was probably nursing a hangover. He looked uncharacteristically unkempt in a loose, rather crumpled check shirt over black jogging bottoms and no shoes or socks. Sienna stretched out her arms and gave him a bear hug, understanding immediately that he was not coping with the possibility of breaking up with Gabrielle.

"Come in, Sienna, and sit down, please."

Sienna hadn't been to Xavier's flat before and entered a rather overcrowded room full of what she termed "paraphernalia". The flat was actually quite nice, but she sensed that recent events had made Xavier lose his customary orderliness. The room was quite modern, with plain white walls interspaced with the occasional modern piece of abstract art or hung ceramic. The grey painted bookshelves were crammed with books (mostly on travel or distant lands, she noted). There were further piles of books on the luxurious-looking Turkish rug and yet more books and papers were strewn about the room – clearly not in their usual habitat. The off-white modern sofa was also scattered with un-ironed shirts, ties and various bits of just-worn clothing.

Xavier was now sitting slumped on the sofa and offered her a coffee he had made in the tiny, jumbled kitchen. *Hmm...this place needs a woman's touch...* thought Sienna. She had never seen Xavier like this. He was a confident, bright and breezy young man who made everyone laugh with his terrible jokes and easy company.

"Xavier," she said softly, "tell me what's happened?" Sienna had a great deal of time for Xavier. Not only had he shown her round so many interesting places in Paris, he had introduced her to people that were becoming good friends, and friendship was important to her. She had a real soft spot for him and was beginning to regard him as the brother she never had. So close had they become as friends, she felt she could confide in him and him with her. There was a trust between them which they both valued...a platonic love which was not defined by romance but by deep friendship.

"Well, Sienna, I really believe it's over with Gabrielle. I don't think either of us can cope any longer with the rows, the silences and the not knowing where it will all end. As you know, my job is so important, and I love it. I love to travel too...and I admit that part of me likes to feel free – free as a little bird, *comme un petit oiseau*. I love her, but I don't think I can make the commitment to the way of life she wants and deserves. Maybe sometime in the future, I will feel the yearning for a family of my own – for children and making a home. For now, I don't feel that – maybe I'm just not cut out for marriage." A tear trickled down his cheek as Sienna put her arm around his shoulder.

"Don't be too hard on yourself, Xavier. I know that your parents have stayed together, but you've seen a lot of rows and bickering between them over the years. It's probably made you a bit mistrustful?"

"I really don't know, Sienna. I just have a strong need at the moment to be my own man."

"Then that's what you must do, Xavier. You are young and intelligent. You have a wonderful career ahead of you and a lot of travel, if that's what you want."

"But she thinks I'm selfish, Sienna…"

"Xavier, you always put others first and that is why everyone loves you! Please make a decision very soon, today even. I think you will then feel better. Gabrielle is clearly unhappy too. Make that phone call when I'm gone and start afresh. Next time when I see you, I want to see your flat sorted out, like the Xavier I know! I'll help you if necessary, but you need to get organised and throw a lot of junk away, along with the junk in your life."

Xavier looked worn out and tired, so Sienna left him smoking a *Gitane* and drinking a fine Cognac.

"I'll ring you tomorrow, Xavier, but you must finish this unhealthy relationship…" With that, Sienna left and made her way to her lecture on Marcel Proust. She quite liked his writing, mercifully.

Chapter Nine

The ring from her shiny, white bedside telephone startled Sienna from a deep slumber and a weird dream of being in a large art gallery in Barcelona. She leaned over wearily to answer it, grabbing the impossible duvet from its topsy-turvy position at the end of her bed.

"*Bonjour, Sienna!*" Lily said brightly.

"Oh, Lily, great to hear from you, but I've just woken up…in fact, I'm not sure if I'm really awake! I'll pop you on hold for a minute if that's ok as I need to go and switch the heating on – it's freezing. Hang on…" Sienna, rather grumpily, crossed the room, grabbing her long, white, fleecy dressing gown and eyed the window. Soft white snowflakes were falling gently outside, and a large puddle had formed on the windowsill, which was desperately in need of attention. Sienna groaned…

"Lily, I'm back, but I feel in a bad mood today…probably the alcohol from last night."

"I've had a modelling assignment cancelled today and wondered if you'd like to meet up and maybe do some shopping? It's just beginning to snow here, though. What do you think?"

Sienna loved fresh snow and the stillness of the air as it fell silently from a loaded sky that promised even more. Sadly, she'd slipped and fallen over on an icy patch several years earlier and hurt her ankle badly. It had taken so long to recover and was so painful that she was now wary of walking on snowy or icy pavements. She explained it to Lily, grabbing a tablet to ease her headache.

"Why don't you come here today, Lily, a bit later on? I'll get us some lunch and we can catch up?"

At that particular moment, she didn't feel like talking to anyone, even Lily who was, as usual, as bright as a button.

"Excellent!" Lily replied.

Lily still lived in the Marais. She'd been there all her life and loved it. She'd watched the old medieval streets come alive over the years and become a really rather *cool* place to live. There were trendy shops and restaurants and the district was becoming popular with a thriving Jewish and gay community. The clubs were young and there was a constant buzz of nightlife. Lily hopped on the Métro and it didn't take long to arrive at Sienna's apartment. The snow was still falling gently on the pavements and covering the rooftops with an icy mantle. The air was bitterly cold – but Lily loved it. Paris could do no wrong. Sienna answered the door to a tiny, but immaculate Lily, huddled in a stunning, belted, warm-looking coat, the collar of which she wore turned up. She was eye-catching with her shiny black bob peeping out of the purple and blue checked coat. Her slender but shapely legs were covered by deep-blue woollen tights that she'd tucked into short lace-up black boots with a grey fur trim. Lily stepped inside, after shaking the snow from her large purple umbrella – which by no coincidence matched the purple in her coat.

The two girls laughed a great deal and giggled over a glass or two of Beaujolais. Despite the earlier hangover, Sienna had deemed it light enough for lunch. They ate a steaming onion soup and baguettes which warmed them both nicely. It was still snowing hard outside and the noise of traffic seemed mainly missing. Paris was rarely so quiet...

"I've so many questions, Lily!" Sienna began. "Is that ok?"

"Of course, *Chérie*! What can I help you with?"
Sienna blushed a little. "I feel so dowdy amongst you Parisian ladies. I have no idea how you all manage to look so chic – in such an effortless way. Also, why are so many people suddenly wearing a lot of electric blue?"

"Ahh..." laughed Lily.

"I was walking into the Jardin du Luxembourg the other day and I espied two ladies – not together. One had a beautiful blue scarf draped over a deep-navy coat and was wearing a large blue ring. Then at the exit, I saw another with a black coat, a neat, blue leather handbag with a chain and a blue beret. She also had a little dog, wearing a blue and grey checked coat! Then, the next day I was at the shops in the Madeleine area and noticed that several of the men were wearing blue scarves and matching blue lace-ups with their dark overcoats. It looked so great – so stylish – but whatever is that all about Lily?"

Lily smiled. "That's Parisians for you. We love to be stylish and à la mode! The men make an effort too."

"Oh, it's fashion?"

"Yes, Sienna, there is often one main colour a lot of people adopt. Last year it was red, and we accessorize with it to bring our classic outfits up to date! But there will be other fashionable colours too…"

"How clever!" Sienna enthused. "So, you don't just go out and buy a blue coat?"

"That's possible too, of course, but then it would probably look dated next year."

Sienna had immediate visions of a shopping spree and she loved that the men here cared how they looked.

"We dress classically, really," continued Lily, "but always with a twist. It might be our own signature – like a large statement ring, a thin scarf tied in an unusual way, a type of necklace like a chunky chain and so on. Then we add our signature perfume and always wear that one…"

"But you're all so tiny! I'm slim, but I've never looked like you lot. I think Parisiennes are secretly on a permanent diet…" Sienna laughed.

"No, not at all," smiled Lily. "But we are careful. We do not snack like the English do. You would never see us walking along the street munching chocolate or crisps or anything really. We take our time and savour it when we eat – and our baguettes are never laden with butter either! Also, we only drink wine with a meal and never to excess. A Parisienne is brought up to look after her skin and complexion too. It's not a treat to have a facial here, you know, our mothers take us to a beautician from the age of fifteen or sixteen. They teach us how to cleanse and moisturise our skin too. *C'est normal en France!*"

"Wow," said Sienna, intrigued by it all. She made a mental note to make a beautician's appointment *tout suite* (right now), remembering how spotty and unattractive she'd felt before going out recently to the *Gypsy Jazz* night. *Hmm… time for a new me!* she decided.

The girls spent several hours laughing and chatting about the latest films (which they both loved), the Parisian art galleries and, most of all, Sienna liked to chat about the people at the Jazz Club.

"I can't believe how caring you all are about each other. Theo has a bad foot, so people fetch him in turn by car, Mireille suffers from panic attacks – but everyone knows, and they seem to take it in turns to help calm her down when necessary."

"Yes, a group of us have known each other for a long time." Sienna sensed that was the end of the subject and went over to the window to see if it was still snowing, before Lily set off home. The snow had stopped, but the puddle on the windowsill was even larger and was beginning to drip onto her putty-coloured rug. She said her goodbyes to Lily, grabbed a large thick towel to mop up some of the water and then remembered she should ring Xavier. Xavier was fine – well, not exactly fine, but the relationship with Gabrielle was over.

"I'm so sorry," Sienna sympathised. "You know, Xavier, it will be hard, but I use a phrase from an old English poem when things are troubling me…*In acceptance lieth peace.*" She then explained what it meant in French.

Chapter Ten

The following day was filled with lectures and tutorials. Luckily, she was prepared for the tutorial. The lecture was in a large, rather cold room at the Sorbonne and the teaching concerned Stendhal and his famous book, *Le Rouge et le Noir*. This was interesting in parts, but Sienna found her mind wandering; she needed to go shopping, should she get her hair cut? Would Ernst be at the Jazz Club on Saturday night?

Saturday took a long time to arrive, but she'd been busy. She looked in the mirror with satisfaction. Her face was delicately made up and blemish-free; in fact, now it seemed to be glowing. She skipped the haircut but found a wonderfully creative hairdresser (via Lily, of course!), who massaged her scalp until it tingled and moisturised her hair until it shone. She then dressed it by partially tying it back and letting the rest fall as loose ringlets, almost to her shoulders. She stepped into her new dress that she'd bought at the big Parisian department store in the 8th arrondissement called Galeries La Fayette. It was in a soft black and was incredibly flattering as it skimmed her slim figure closely. Her shiny natural stockings were worn with deep-blue suede kitten heels (well, something had to be blue, didn't it?). She wore a simple black coat with a belt over the dress. Lily was driving to the club that evening and stopped off to pick up Sienna.

"Sienna, you look A-M-A-Z-I-N-G!" she exclaimed. "Quite the little Parisienne, eh?" Sienna blushed with delight and re-applied some lipstick as they approached the club. They knocked on the now familiar door and a musician, clasping a clarinet to his chest like a lover, opened it up.

"*Entrez! Entrez, mes amis!* said the man on the door. It was already the interval as they had been held back by the still icy roads. They made for the bar, ordered some drinks and looked around.

"*Bonsoir! Bonsoir!*" Alphonse and Mireille were talking together, Theo chatted to the intellectual-looking chap (*What was his name…?*) that Sienna had seen with the lady called Hélène, who had the long plait. Freya was missing – Sienna sighted someone else she knew…but no Ernst! With a crestfallen look, Sienna sank into one of the velvety chairs and the music started up again. It was a "clarinet night" and she recognised a lot of the sultry tones of the renowned Jazz musicians.

"Sienna!" Alphonse exclaimed "You look wonderful! *Tres belle ce soir!*" ("Very beautiful tonight!")

"*Merci, Alphonse…*"

"Shall we dance?"

Sienna moved forward and danced slowly with Alphonse. She was aware that people were looking at them – and she felt good. As the music stopped, ready to launch into something different, she felt a tap on her shoulder. She turned around to see the smiling face of Ernst.

"You look sensational, Sienna," he cooed as he placed his arm around her waist. "I'm late because I had to take Freya to hospital. She had cut herself on an old iron side-table she'd bought today, which was unexpectedly sharp in places. She's OK now thankfully. Sienna, I have thought about you so much this week. Shall we do this slow dance together? It's Sidney Bechet's "*Petite Fleur*" – do you know it? It's one of my favourites. I didn't realise the saxophonist had taken over for the rest of the evening…"

Ernst led her forward to where a handful of couples were dancing, slowly and sensuously to the music. He held her close, looking deeply with his soulful brown eyes into hers. Her skin tingled with excitement, as she held his gaze and moved dreamily to the beat of the music.

"Sienna, you always look amazing…but tonight even more so!" She stared, almost unbelievingly at his perfect face and his inviting lips, as the music stopped, and he led her back to a small, soft and inviting little chaise longue. As Ernst sat down, Sienna eyed his body for the first time. His face was very Gallic. He had a strong jaw and quite high cheekbones. His skin was a deep olive hue and would surely be very tanned in summer. He was of athletic build – muscular, without looking like he hit the gym on a daily basis. She had already noticed his small pert buttocks and long well-toned legs.

"Sienna…" he said softly, "I need to ask you something. I have to go soon as I've promised to get back to keep an eye on Freya, who's not feeling too well. Next week I'm going away for a day outside Paris, near a beautiful forest, where I was born. It's so peaceful there – away from the crowds here in Paris. I was wondering if you'd like to come with me?" Sienna replied that she'd love to come with him and secretly felt happier than she had in a long, long time.

Chapter Eleven

Mireille sat alone at the tiny bistro near the Champs-Élysées. She cut a rather lonely figure against the groups of people all huddled outside and chatting animatedly. The weather was cold as it was November, but Mireille had felt the need to be out and indulge in a bit of people-watching. The snow had long gone but the sky had a gloomy cloak of uninviting grey cloud and threatened rain. Oh, for the summer! She sighed and drank her steaming coffee pensively. More friends – was that the answer? A new romance? The phone didn't seem to ring so much nowadays and, as she wasn't working at present, some days seemed interminable. She still danced as beautifully as ever, moving across the stage in a graceful, controlled but exquisite manner. Her *Folies Bergère* days were long gone, but she made ends meet by dancing on temporary assignments in the city. Right now, however, her agent said there was no work available. Mireille thought about her life. Her parents had come to Paris from Algeria when she was a child. It was originally a holiday, but they never went back. Her father worked in, and eventually bought, a little bar in the Montmartre area. Mireille was used to the Parisian night-life as a child and always loved to dance. This led her to her present career, which she still enjoyed. Her parents were now retired and lived in Nice, so she saw little of them and it was somewhat lonely. She had a group of friends – the main one being her beloved Theo, who owned the little art shop in the Latin Quarter. They met up at the Jazz Club each Saturday but would often talk on the phone several times a week. How she loved Theo – though he wasn't interested in romance with a woman, Mireille adored him. There was a phase a few years back when she really believed they were in love and that Theo could "undo" his sexuality. It didn't happen. Theo knew but was amazingly gentle with her, as always.

"My dear Mireille, *ma Chérie…*" he had said softly. "It can never *be* – you and me – but know that I love you dearly and our friendship is so important to me. I will always be there for you. I would like us to continue having fun together and being close." And so, it was. She admired Theo for his artistic and individualistic nature, the way he dressed and his optimistic outlook on life. She understood the pride that he took in selling his quality artist materials. He loved art and so did she. They would spend many an afternoon together wandering around the galleries in Paris and talking excitedly about the differing styles of painting, the unusual use of sepia ink and watercolours and so on. Sometimes Lily or Alphonse would join them, and they'd have lunch together and make a day of it. *Theo*, Mireille thought, *is such a gentle soul and very insightful.* She knew she could tell him absolutely anything and he would use his deep intuition to help her through any problems that had occurred in her colourful love life! There were a few occasions where she had arrived on his doorstep in tears. They would go out and wander around the Marais, often stopping for a drink at a bar in the area's thriving gay community. Mireille loved it when Lily came too, as she valued her advice.

"Ah, Lily…! How I wish I was as elegant and beautiful as her!" she would say to Theo, a tad enviously. Occasionally, Mireille suffered panic attacks at a Jazz session and Lily was always quick to take her to an adjacent quiet room and hold her hand until she felt better. Her mood lifted slightly as she thought about her dear friends and how lucky she was.

Mireille decided to get a taxi over to Saint Germain, as the Métro gave her panic attacks. She went to see Freya, who would be at the shop and no doubt would have some *objets trouvés* (finds) to show her from her latest travels around the flea markets. There was usually a bit of girly gossip to catch up on and today was no exception. The two girls embraced and sat down to a cup of English tea and delicious flat, chocolate-covered cakes, with exquisite iced designs on them.

"*Eh bien, Mireille.* So, did you see Ernst and Sienna at the Jazz Club?"

"Of course," replied Mireille, "and she looked lovely! They are going to make a wonderful couple."

Chapter Twelve

When you have a large, old English grandfather clock in the corner of the room, the constant ticking makes time seem to move more slowly somehow —or is it just reminding me that the days are dragging? Sienna mused. There was only one thing on her mind and that was a call from Ernst. She was surrounded by papers – essays she had yet to finish about Jean-Paul Sartre and notes she'd jotted down yesterday at the lecture on George Sand (*Was he really a woman?*) and lots of reminders scattered over her putty-coloured rug; an assortment of food- shopping lists, phone numbers and things to do. *However did I get into this mess?* The answer came back swiftly and clearly: her concentration was clearly elsewhere…

In order to restore some semblance of normality, she put her coat on and went off to the *boucherie* where Monsieur Martin would sell her some tender chicken to make *coq au vin*.

"Bonjour, Sienna!"

"Bonjour, Monsieur Martin, ça va? I need some *poulet* (chicken) for my *coq au vin* and some of this exotic-looking *saucisson* – What is it?"

"It has garlic and spices, Sienna. Would you like to try a piece?"

It was, of course, delicious. Everything in the *boucherie* had been lovingly hung, cut and arranged by Monsieur Martin. Everyone knew him, and he had an excellent reputation. Sienna loved the way the shopkeepers in France took such pride in their wares. They greeted everyone by name and she'd learned as a tourist – years back – that it was expected of you to greet them with a warm *Bonjour!* It was so refreshing after some of her shops at home where the owners barely looked up from their newspapers when someone entered the shop, or sometimes just stood and gossiped. Satisfied with her purchase, she set off home only to hear the phone ringing loudly as she reached her door. She practically ran to the phone and pressed the receiver hopefully to her ear.

"Sienna!" a soft voice said. "I thought you weren't there – It's Ernst…I hope you remember me!" She laughed, happily, trying to disguise the fact that her stomach had just done a total somersault and her legs felt strangely weak.

"Would you like to come with me to Milly-La-Forêt tomorrow? My mother lives there and you will love it. We can also visit some of the nearby places of interest and walk in the forest, so bring some sturdy boots and wrap up well, eh?"

"Will do, Ernst – when will you pick me up?"

"Well, let's set off early so we can have plenty of time and savour the day. I will be there at eight-thirty. Is that too soon?" *Too soon!* thought Sienna. *He must be joking…*

She skipped through to the kitchen to make her *coq au vin* and plan what to wear the next day.

"Thank you! Thank you, God!" She smiled. Sienna wasn't really religious, but it was always good to be thankful, just in case He was listening…

Chapter Thirteen

Sienna was up early, at "silly o'clock" as she called it. She took a shower, putting on all sorts of luxurious oils and finally her new light perfume by Roger and Gallet, with delicious lemon undertones. She grabbed a plump croissant and some black coffee and then dressed for the cold. She put on a thick, light-grey jumper over her dark grey jeans, which she tucked into her short fleece-lined boots, which were snug and warm. The next layer was her padded charcoal waterproof jacket, topped with a long, warm, pink woollen scarf which she wrapped several times around her neck. She had tied her hair up and pulled on a deep-pink woollen hat, which showed off her pretty, round face, yet would help fend off the cold. Armed with her large, black leather tote, she grabbed some gloves and a flask of warm drink, placing them in the bag, and ran to the door. Ernst had just pulled up outside with the familiar creak and clunk of his little car. He kissed Sienna on the cheek, lovingly. Sienna saw that he was warmly attired in a thick, navy three-quarter-length "pea coat", blue jeans and boots plus a navy beanie pulled down slightly over those large, sad brown eyes. She gulped...

"It's crisp weather, Sienna! The sun is shining, though, and it doesn't threaten to snow today." He took the wheel and pulled off. "It's a bit of a journey, but first of all I'd like us to drive to Rambouillet; I was born there. It's a beautiful little town, just outside Paris, with its very own *château*. I hope that's ok?"

"Oh yes," she replied, thinking, *anything would be ok!* "It will be good to have a break from the noise of the city, get some exercise... and to spend the day with you..." *Did that sound too keen?*

It was quite a way so would take about an hour and a half, but Sienna loved the open French countryside as they passed through. The bare winter landscape stood waiting expectantly for spring. The November sunshine, however, darted through the leafless trees and held the promise of a blaze of colour from the little plants beneath, which were hiding from the biting wind. Ernst passed Sienna a thick tartan rug that had belonged to his maternal grandmother. He wanted her to be warm and cosy as they stopped for a drink from her flask. In doing so, he brushed her knee with his hand and Sienna smiled across, thanking him for his thoughtfulness. They arrived at Rambouillet and parked near to the *Château*. For a while they wandered the cobbled streets, hand in hand. It was a quiet, pretty little town.

"This is where I was born," said Ernst. "Rue de la Motte."

"Moat road?" asked Sienna. "Must be near the castle."

"I was actually born in this house," he pointed to a rather quaint-looking building. "Fortunately, the midwife lived on this road too. Come, let's go and see the *Château*." The small Château de Rambouillet was picturesque and compact. Ernst explained that it had been used by several presidents over the years for conferences and the like. The gardens, parks and walkways were lovely: planted with beautiful trees – now bare, but still striking – and rows of twigs and plants out of which the heads of delicate, colourful flowers would pop up expectantly when Spring showed signs of arriving the next year. The air was sharp and bracing, but they were oblivious as they enjoyed each other's company.

Sienna took his arm and they cuddled close against the cold as they walked. They turned a corner in the magnificent gardens by a lake where no one else was around; they felt like they were the only two people on Earth, alone, apart from a feisty little robin. Ernst took Sienna's chilly face in his hands, gently, and leaned in to kiss her soft lips. They shared their first kiss, their faces glowing in the winter air.

"Sienna, I really care about you, you know. You are a beautiful girl and I hope we can share many more kisses?" Sienna murmured in agreement as he kissed her parted lips with passion this time.

"Come on!" Ernst said. "It's so cold – let's get back to the car and drive to Milly-La-Forêt, to see my mother." Sienna didn't want the perfect day to ever end.

Chapter Fourteen

Milly-La-Forêt turned out to be a beautiful little market town not too far from Rambouillet, nestling at the edge of the forest and situated to the north of Paris. Ernst explained that his parents fell in love with it years previously, but when his father died a few years back, his mother, wanting to leave Paris and their memories, moved here. There was a wonderful architectural heritage in the town, where an old, wooden, covered market dating back to the fifteenth century was still held. His mother loved to go to the market. As they walked along, hand in hand, Ernst pointed out Le Chateau de la Bonde– with its two towers either side – and, as they crossed over a stone bridge over the river, he showed Sienna an old picturesque wash- house.

"*Maman* loves it here, and you can see why! There is plenty of interesting history here which fascinates her, a lot of things that date back to the Middle Ages. See – we are now walking through a beautiful herb garden around the chapel. *Maman* collects the herbs to make natural medicines. It used to be a speciality in Milly during the Middle Ages, so now she is carrying on a tradition – in a small way, of course..."

"How fascinating, Ernst! I'm quite interested in herbal medicine and think we rely too much on drugs, which are not always the answer."

Madame LaFargue was having a nap in her little cottage as the couple approached. They had left the car in the town and walked towards the forest, along a fairly isolated track, to where she lived. Ernst knocked on the door, softly, using its old-fashioned, wrought-iron knocker and it was not long before his mother opened the door.

"Ernst! *Mon fils*!" ("My son!") she kissed him lovingly. "And you must be Sienna? I can speak a little English. I am so pleased to meet you!" she said with a strong French accent. "Please do come inside and be warm."

Sienna took an instant liking to her. Madame LaFargue was a warm, youthful-looking lady in her sixties. She wore her almost-white hair in a bob and had today pushed it back at the front with a bandeau of pink floral fabric. She had always loved clothes and fashion – and it showed. She was wearing a pale denim shirt and jeans, which was more-or-less her go-to daily attire, as she pottered around her cottage and garden and industriously blended her herbal mixtures in the kitchen. She seemed happy.

"Come through, Sienna!" Madame LaFargue had reverted back to French now as her school-girl English was very limited. "Would you like a warm drink? Maybe something to eat? You two must be pretty cold…"

They walked through a small hallway with a mottled stone floor and Sienna immediately sensed the cosiness that lay within. She passed an oak console table in the hall which had a few interesting and – probably treasured – objects on it: an old vase, a stone jug and an unusually shaped metal pitcher in a dull steel colour. They were carefully placed to blend with each other. As they moved on into the sitting room, Sienna admired the simplicity and understated look of the décor. The unplastered and bare stone walls did not look cold; they complimented the room which was warmly decorated in a rural, rustic style in soft ochres and sage greens. The curtains were made from striped ticking and blended in with the other natural materials, all in subdued shades. There were a few terracotta pots, which reminded Sienna of the Jazz Club and had the same sensuous warmth about them. Large and small plump cushions in simple shapes and made from old and new fabrics adorned the plain but comfy sofa. Some of these were in striped or patterned material, others in plain sumptuous velvet. A soft, thick dusky-pink rug lived in front of the sofa. Sienna's eye finally wandered across the room to a large, bronze standard lamp; a delicately patterned floral lampshade sat tilted on its metal stand. Sienna resisted the temptation to straighten it! She was bowled over. *This has been furnished with a great deal of thought and love*, she thought, as she sank into the sumptuous sofa with Ernst and drank tea, accompanied by delicate shortbreads and tiny cakes.

"*Maman*, may I go and check out the garden?" Ernst asked in a boyish tone.

"Of course, but there is little to see at this time of year and it's cold, so don't stay out too long." Ernst had only been gone a short time when his mother rushed to the door and ushered him in. He was wheezing uncontrollably and trying to catch his breath.

"Stay there, Sienna. I know what to do..." said his mother. She ran to his coat and found an inhaler which she passed to Ernst, who by now was sitting on the sofa next to Sienna.

"I told you, Ernst. It's too cold for you!" said Madame LaFargue. "Here, drink this sweet herbal tea and rest a while." As Ernst regained his composure and began to breath in a regular manner, his mother explained what was going on to Sienna.

"Ernst has asthma, which he has had since he was a child. It got worse a few years ago when his father suddenly died. Ernst became very agitated by the whole affair. See, he's fine now!"

Sienna wondered what happened to make him so agitated when his father died, but when she tried to ask, Madame LaFargue explained about her herbs and the remedies she made from them.

"Do you sell them?" Sienna enquired.

"Yes, I have someone from whom I buy herbs in a neighbouring town. They are often from Provence... the famous *Herbes de Provence*, but also many others which are medicinal and not for cooking. In fact, my friend will be here soon with her car and, if you don't mind, I will pop out and deliver some remedies to the young girl who sells them on a stall for me. I couldn't brave this weather on foot! Ernst, take this tincture, please. It's blended especially for you. Sienna, do make sure he takes it, please! Ernst can be forgetful sometimes, if not a little stubborn."

"I wonder where I got that from...?" Ernst retorted with a laugh. As he rested with some of his mother's favourite Aznavour music in the background, his mother led Sienna through into her busy kitchen, of which she was so proud.

It was a typically French-style kitchen, not with fitted units but with individual cupboards of varying sizes placed here and there. The sink was a deep-blue, speckled enamel bowl and there was a cupboard beneath with a small, blue-checked curtain across it. The room housed all sorts of jars, pots and pans, bottles, container and utensils – the like and variety Sienna had never seen. It led out onto what was surely a delightful garden in summer. She could imagine it with its sweet-smelling flowers and herbs. Although at present it was rather bare and forlorn, it seemed full of promise. Sienna espied lots of pots: some cracked by the frost, some intact. There were a few deep-brown metal containers that looked like old milk churns (but probably weren't) and grey, metal, conical buckets, some of which were used for dried flowers in the kitchen. In the corner of the small garden was an old, dilapidated metal chair with painted – but chipped – wooden slats and scrolled metal arms. It sat comfortably in one corner, overlooking a pond with a brick-edging and, at present, covered in algae.

"How interesting!" Sienna remarked. "I imagine this looks stunning when all the flowers are out as well as the climbing plants on the fences."

"It's actually very peaceful too, Sienna." Madame LaFargue smiled. "I often grab a cushion and sit in the sunshine, reading or just dreaming. Dreaming is good for the soul, don't you think?"

Madame LaFargue showed Sienna a row of neatly arranged glass jars and bottles, all carefully labelled in exquisite calligraphy in black ink.

"My husband wrote beautifully, you see. Since he died I've taken over the labelling job and learned to write like him. Look, Sienna – this one's called *Sureau* here in

France." Sienna quickly took out her pocket dictionary for enlightenment.

"Ah, it's elderberry!"

"This plant is not exactly an herb," continued Madame LaFargue. "It has been held in high respect since Celtic times. It is powerful for colds and flu, so very useful at this time of year..." She moved onto a bottle of rosemary. "It's a really useful herb and is good for things like digestion after a heavy meal." The next blue bottle was labelled *Thyme*.

"I use that in cooking!" said Sienna.

"Indeed, but it's an antiseptic and useful for colds, sore throats and coughs too. I will just show you my sage. I use it as a stomach tonic and it helps to strengthen my gums. Now my dear, I won't detain you any longer with my ramblings. I have to leave in five minutes as a friend is collecting me by car." Sienna thanked her for showing her the remedies and they went back to the sitting room where Ernst had nodded off on the sofa.

"I'm off now – I hear the door. Back in around an hour..." and with that Madame LaFargue disappeared.
Sienna kissed Ernst gently on the cheek and he stirred.

"Ah... come here, Sienna..." as he folded her into his outstretched arms. "*Maman* will be gone a while and I'm going to kiss you until we can no longer continue!"

"Mmm..." murmured Sienna and nestled up to him on the sofa. Ernst pulled her close and they kissed passionately. Ernst caressed the back of her neck whilst Sienna lay back and enjoyed his advances.

"Sienna, you smell fantastic..." The aroma of her perfume heightened Ernst's passion. He took her hand and kissed one of her knuckles. Sienna was feeling aroused by his sensuous touches.

"Sienna, I want to make love with you here...now!" Sienna didn't know how to reply. She kissed him gently on his nose and said, "Ernst, of course, I feel the same, but we hardly know each other, and it has to be an act of love for me...please, can we wait?"
Ernst pulled back, smiling.

"Of course, Sienna, I understand...and how would we explain the ruffled cushions and creased sofa to my mother!" he laughed. They decided to go for a walk and wandered around outside together, hand-in-hand and laughing. They kicked the leaves on the pathway through the trees, just on the edge of the forest. The leaves danced in the wind and courted each other as they were blown together in a melange of burnt oranges, browns and russet golds. Sienna looked up at Ernst happily and saw his smiling eyes – for the rest of his face was hidden by a thick, grey mohair scarf. It occurred to her that it was beginning to get dark and a bit colder, and she didn't want Ernst to have another asthma attack, so they made their way back, just as Madame LaFargue returned. Not going inside, Ernst said, "*Maman, merci!* We've had such a lovely time here, but I think we should head back to Paris before it's dark." Madame LaFargue kissed them both on the cheek.

"*Au revoir*, Sienna!" she said, warmly. "Please look after Ernst and make sure he takes my tincture..." Sienna nodded, and they made their way back to the car.

"The end of a perfect day!" she said, lovingly, to Ernst.

"You're fantastic, Sienna. You've made me so happy..." he replied, squeezing her hand.

Sienna arrived home to a message from Xavier on her answerphone. He sounded good and after having a quick meal, she returned his call.

"*Xavier, comment ça va, mon cher?*" ("Xavier, how are you, my friend?")

Xavier replied that he was fine, though he'd had some really bad days but had quickly came to the conclusion that it was the best thing that could have happened, splitting from Gabrielle – it just wouldn't have worked out.

"Are you eating well and looking after yourself?"

"Oh yes, Sienna, don't worry – and I've even started tidying the place up!" Feeling relieved, Sienna told him about her day out with Ernst. Xavier had espied them together at the Jazz Club.

"I'm just so happy, Xavier," she cooed. "Ernst is wonderful and I'm so comfortable in his company."

"Well, Sienna, I'm pleased you have someone to carry on showing you around Paris, as I don't need the money any more to get to Barcelona, so I'm retiring from my duties..."

"That's great, Xavier – you were looking rather tired and jaded. Overwork is not good for the soul. A new beginning for the both of us, eh? I do hope we can stay close friends and call and see each other often."

"That goes without saying, my lovely Sienna," he replied, "but do take care, please."

"Why do you say that, Xavier?" Sienna was puzzled.

"Oh, it's just that..." Xavier laughed, "you are a young, innocent girl in the big city that is Paris."

"Oh, don't worry about me now!" Sienna laughed.

"I'm sure Ernst will look after me. Speak soon, eh?" With that, she put the phone down and put on one of her favourite Jazz tracks – "Saint Louis Blues" – as she poured herself another glass of Merlot and sank back into the cushions, dreamily.

Everything is perfect. Just perfect, she mused. *Tomorrow I have no lectures, so I think I will go shopping for some elegant undies. After all, Lily has told me I should always wear something matching and attractive, even on a day-to-day basis, as it's good for the self-confidence and makes you feel extra special. Well, that's what the Parisiennes do, so I will too!* She laughed as she thought of her mother's attitude towards lingerie.

"Now come on, Sienna," she had told her when she became a teenager. *"You must always make sure you wear clean knickers under your clothes – just in case you're in an accident!"*

"The English...!" sighed Sienna, as she lay back and indulged in her silent reverie. She wondered when she would see Ernst again and how long it would be before she felt ready to make love with him. Having finished her wine, she dreamily wandered towards the bedroom, wishing he were there...

Chapter Fifteen

Alphonse looked out of the window in horror. The rain was pelting down outside and forming large puddles on the sill. *Time to get the guttering sorted*, he sighed. It was blustery and *dank*. "Dank" happened to be a favourite description of his to describe a day such as this: wet, cold and dark.

"Well, that's me inside for the day. No takers today!" Alphonse, true to Sienna's first impression, was now an artist. As Christmas was fast approaching, he was hoping to sell a few more paintings. Alphonse had originally been a regular in Montmartre, where many talented artists painted outside to sell to the eager tourists. He'd made quite a lot of money, especially from the Americans. However, in recent years he had sold his art (mostly prints) along the Left Bank, across from Notre Dame. It was a pleasant site and Notre Dame attracted a lot of tourists all year round who would come over to where he was and buy his paintings and prints.

"*Zut alors!*" he muttered and sat down with a coffee and a book he was reading about Picasso. The phone rang; it was Lily.

"*Bonjour, Lily! Il pleut aujourd hui, eh?*" ("Hello, Lily! It's raining today, eh?")

"Are you OK, Alphonse?"

"No, I'm not," he replied. Alphonse was, of course, Lily's brother, and they adored each other. They had always been close but even more so now that their parents had died. He loved his beautiful sister.

"Is it money again, Alphonse?"

"*Mais oui!* I'm not selling much at the moment, Lily..." he said, kicking the rug desolately, with his old leather boot. Now Lily, of course, had a wonderful career as a model, which still brought in quite a lot of work. She often gave Alphonse money on a "permanent loan". Alphonse had a typical artist's atelier with a small kitchen and bedroom beneath in Saint Germain. When he struggled with his rent, Lily would help. Everybody loved Alphonse, as he was a placid, gentle soul, who was very unmaterialistic and required little to keep him happy. When money was tight, he would still be seen tossing coins to street beggars and chatting amiably to them. If it was extra cold and they were shivering, he would fetch a hot chocolate and thick blanket. He valued his good friends and often met up with Mireille as she too had little work nowadays. There had been a brief romance between them, but it hadn't worked out – Mireille was difficult – however, they maintained a strong friendship. He loved the Jazz Club, where he was often seen laughing at the bar with Theo or Xavier and mingling with everyone. People would buy him a beer as they knew his situation and he was well liked. Today would be another day of painting. Alphonse was very innovative with his ideas. He decided to finish a large canvas which, if successful, he was going to sell in a gallery.

The atelier lent itself well to creativity. The light, streaming through the overhead skylight, was ideal for his work. The walls were painted in a pale, minty-green chalk paint and, here and there, he'd hung his quite dramatic paintings. There was a young-ish lady who he'd sketched in inks and washed over with bright watercolours. She looked Spanish with her olive skin and black shiny hair pulled back in a bun. She was a Flamenco dancer that Alphonse had sketched on a trip to Spain. She wore a bright-red low-neck dress with a frill, and she was looking over her shoulder with attitude. Alphonse was considering taking her to the gallery. Other paintings were mostly scenic: sunlight flickering on the Seine, an old barge passing by the crowded bank near Notre Dame, and a lovely scene of eager, jostling tourists on the 'Rue Mouffetard' (a famous street in Saint Germain with a wonderful food market). He'd sold quite a few prints of these, mostly to Americans. He sat on an old sofa, now covered with a cloth that had paint marks on it. The atmosphere was bohemian! He had a couple of easels – which were both in use, a paint-stained cloth lay on the floor and several little wooden tables were scattered around bearing all manner of brushes in jam jars, acrylic paints in tubes, along with tubes of watercolour. There were also pencils and sticks of charcoal laid out carefully and a set of oils which he rarely used as it wasn't his favourite medium.

Last week, Alphonse had sketched a model who was a friend of Lily's. It wasn't a nude sketch, but she was wearing a very low silky dress and was in a quite seductive pose. He was hopeful that this would be a masterpiece! It was again a large canvas and Alphonse had set to, skilfully using his watercolours in a very loose manner to create an impression rather than a detailed painting. While the paint was still wet, he had added other soft hues of blue and violet to the dusty pink of the dress. The face had just a suggestion of dainty features. He sat down after a few hours, pleased with his effort. Maybe another couple of days work and it would be completed. The phone rang again: it was Sienna. Alphonse had got to know her quite well over the weeks at the club and he was very fond of her.

"Alphonse, please come soon, I need your help. It's Ernst. I'm at his flat, Freya is out, and he can't breathe properly. We have been to the hospital, but there was nothing more to be done. He had to use his inhaler and relax, and all would be well…eventually. But I'm frightened, Alphonse, as he's in such a dark place emotionally!"

Alphonse ran downstairs and got quickly into his old car, which, although on its last legs, got him from A-to-B successfully enough. He was soon chez Ernst. He knew that Sienna and Ernst were an item and felt saddened that this health issue had happened. Indeed, Sienna had gone around for a cup of tea, after her class, hoping for some precious time with him again.

Ernst was seated in an easy chair with his head in his hands. Clearly his breathing had at least returned to normal.

"It's the nightmares, Alphonse," he said despondently. "My father is dying, and I can't help. The next day my asthma is there, and I feel so depressed..."

"Sienna, make some tea would you, my dear?" Alphonse asked. He talked to Ernst in a man-to-man fashion and tried to calm him down.

"I know that you haven't got over the tragic accident your father died in, but it wasn't your fault, Ernst. For your mother's, and now Sienna's, sake, you have got to be strong. It was many years ago now, *mon Cher*. Come on now, look at this beautiful young woman you have..." he said, as Sienna came back with chamomile tea and biscuits.

"Have this chamomile tea. Your mother told you it would help, *n'est ce pas?*"

Ernst rallied round, as the chamomile tea and Alphonse's words had clearly helped. They chatted for a while, then Alphonse left, giving Sienna a lift home too.

"Don't worry, Sienna. He is often like this, I'm afraid, but having you will be his best Christmas present ever!"

Christmas! thought Sienna. *It is already December – I must get organised.* She was going back to England to her parents for a few days but hadn't yet told Ernst.

Chapter Sixteen

The Christmas atmosphere had arrived in Paris. Sienna found it very different to Christmas at home. Here, she had a small, tasteful tree, adorned with only white lights and round, silver matte baubles. Her trees at home had always been piled, willy-nilly, with all manner of decorations and lights that they'd gathered over the years. There were usually a total miss-match of shapes and colours and it now seemed very unstylish, compared to the Parisian tasteful simplicity. She loved the French style, which was always so simple and uncomplicated. Sienna had once read a book by Audrey Hepburn who had stated, "Paris is always a good idea, and especially at Christmas!" She decided to go off on her own and explore the city. First of all, she went over to the Boulevard Haussmann, which was in the 8th arrondissement. Two of Paris's great department stores were here...and what a feast awaited her eyes. The shops were magnificently decked out with lights and stunning ornaments, with rather extravagant decorations, immaculately placed. The colourful window displays grabbed her attention as the big stores competed in the most imaginative display!

Sienna had never seen anything quite like this in London and, inside them, she found a wonderful selection of older and contemporary lights, baubles, trimmings and all manner of decorations which were, of course, unusual yet tasteful. She bought a few select items for the flat, thinking it would be transformed by the gleaming silver. *Should she invite her friends over for a Christmas soirée before she went home?* She stopped off at one of the many street markets but resisted the ice-rinks and other displays in the city, which she could admire on the television later in the day.

"*Ernst, bonjour, mon Cher!*" she said on the phone to her beau. Ernst was always delighted to hear her happy, rather sexy voice; it was music to his ears, with its attractive English accent and her dancing tones. "I'm thinking of having a little Christmas soirée here...I've bought the most wonderful decorations!" she said, excitedly. "It's only three weeks before Christmas. Shall we do it?"

"Sienna, my darling, that sounds amazing – but I would also like a little soirée with just the two of us!" came the reply.

"Of course, Ernst. I'm sorry we haven't spent much time alone since we went to Milly, but I've had so many deadlines with my essays as it's near the end of term, and you were unwell too. Are you okay now?"

Ernst reassured her that he was feeling much better and they agreed that on Friday evening, which was only two days away, he would come over and help put up the decorations and plan the evening ahead with her.

"So, you've seen Paris this week, Sienna? It's so beautiful, isn't it? You can see why it's called the *City of Light*..."

"Oh yes!" answered Sienna. "Absolutely magical. I've never seen anything so surreal!"

She sat down and composed a list of people to invite. *Now, let's see, there's Alphonse, Lily, Theo, Freya, Mireille, Monsieur Martin the butcher and his wife – oh and Xavier, of course. Who else now? Ah, Mireille's friends – the Peruvian lady with the long plait and her companion, the chap with the dark-rimmed glasses. Now what were their names? Then, there's Didier and Patrice – the two waiters at the* Bôite de Jazz. *Patricia and Sylvie, who are my friends at the Sorbonne class, and, of course, Ernst and myself.* She concluded that that would be quite enough to squeeze into her little apartment.

She waited excitedly for Friday. At last she heard the familiar *chug, chug* and slight rattle of Ernst's rather old little car as he pulled up outside and, within minutes, they were in each other's arms again, kissing on the doorstep as though they were the only two people in the world.

"Come in, Ernst. We've so much to organise. I've put a meal in the oven but, for now, let's make a plan. We need to think of food and drink for the guests and also background music for the soirée. *D'accord?* I've also done a list of people and arranged to borrow some comfy chairs from the lady in the flat upstairs."

"*Parfait!*" exclaimed Ernst. "And I see you've already put up the decorations without me!" He didn't seem too pleased at that. "However," Ernst explained, "the French usually do dinner parties and I think we have too many people and not enough room. I have an idea. Let me book a good restaurant nearby and ask if the guests would be prepared to pay for their meal. After that, we could come back for more drinks, coffee and late-night music."

"Oh, a much better idea, Ernst! So, if you can find the restaurant, I will send out invitations at once, so we can book – although I don't know if Alphonse and Mireille would be able to afford it." *Ernst was usually right about things,* Sienna thought, a tad reluctantly.

Ernst picked up the phone to call Lily. *Yes! She would love to come, and she would even be willing to pay for Alphonse and Mireille.*

"I'll sort it tomorrow, Sienna, but for the moment, let's eat and enjoy each other, eh?"

Sienna was getting the knack of French cooking, albeit slowly, and served a delicious evening meal for them both. They sat down in the soft, flickering candlelight at her table, which she'd covered in a crisp white tablecloth. The plates were in a slate-blue colour with matching white napkins, adorned delicately at each corner of the cloth with a slate-blue flower. The glasses were large, rounded wine glasses, which looked like they could hold an awful lot of wine at once, but – being in France – it would be poured out sparingly and savoured…with more to come, of course. The cutlery was bought on her recent trip to the shops and consisted of several large, silver serving spoons, which shone vibrantly in the dim candlelight, and knives and forks, again in silver but with a grey mottled "bone" handles. The tall, white candle was the only light in the room, apart from the deep-brown metal lamp, with its burnt-orange floppy shade, that sat in the corner. Sienna loved the effect of candlelight: *It's so flattering on the face and will be sure to hide that pesky little spot that appeared on my forehead this morning!*

They chatted animatedly sipping the small cocktail aperitif. Now Sienna produced a warm, mixed vegetable soup which she had prepared earlier in the day.

"*Mmm, c'est délicieux, Sienna!*" ("Mmm, it's delicious, Sienna!") Ernst exclaimed, as she went to the kitchen and returned with what the French call *le plat principal*. She'd made a *cassoulet* for the main course: a warm and hearty dish which was rich and slowly cooked in a casserole dish, containing meat, pork skin and white beans. She served it in a *cassole* – a deep earthenware pot, used traditionally to serve the dish in.

"*Du vin?*" she enquired of Ernst.

The wine was chosen (with some help from Alphonse) to go well with the *cassoulet*. It was a *Côtes du Roussillon*: a bright red wine, which was light but fresh enough to offset the richness of the meal. Dessert was a delicious apple tart. After this, they retired to the sofa and had a small coffee as they listened to *"Almost Blue"* by Chet Baker– one of Ernst's favourite Jazz trumpeters, who played moody, romantic music. Ernst nibbled Sienna's ear playfully, while stroking her arm tenderly.

"I have to tell you," murmured Ernst, "that I fear I am falling in love with you...slowly but surely." Sienna looked into his soulful brown eyes and smiled.

"Do I need to reply to that, Ernst?"

She was feeling the same, of course, but found it somewhat scary. He pulled her close and kissed her passionately, loosening the buttons of her silky, soft-pink blouse and caressing the top of her pert breasts, firstly with a gentle hand and then covering them with gentle kisses. He moved towards her with arms outstretched and, lifting her body gently, carried her to the bedroom, her hair tousled and flowing across her shoulder and her shoes now kicked off on the rug. He lay her down gently onto her white, embroidered bedspread and turned on just one small bedside lamp which gave out a dim, dusky light.

Ernst swiftly undressed Sienna, kissing every part of her body as he revealed it. He stroked her neck as she helped him undress, and then she ran her fingers through his hair and down his spine, which prompted a gasp from him. They explored each other's bodies and made love passionately until they rolled over and laughed in delight. Ernst with tousled hair and catching his breath, Sienna with flushed cheeks and a broad smile that displayed the dimple Ernst adored.

"I shall stay here now, *Chérie*, and we will make love all night long..." Ernst whispered.

When the sound of the first birds twittering and cooing started outside and the light of day began to appear here and there through the curtains, they were both fast asleep in each other's arms. At around nine, Sienna stirred, kissed Ernst, and made delicious croissants and jam with steaming hot chocolate, which she brought to the bed on a white tray.

The phone rang.

"Sienna, it's Alphonse," a voice said, excitedly. "I have some news. I've sold my Flamenco lady for an unbelievable amount of money! I just had to tell you!"

"What lovely news!" Sienna replied. *It couldn't have happened to a nicer person.*

"I'm going to take another picture to the gallery today too!"

She told Ernst who was delighted; he had a lot of time for Alphonse. Ernst tugged at Sienna's dressing gown.

"Come back to bed," he whispered.

Chapter Seventeen

Christmas was approaching, and Ernst was feeling disappointed that he would not be able to spend it with Sienna. He understood that she needed to see her parents, but that didn't help. He would drive to Milly-La-Forêt and spend it with *Maman* and a few other relatives. Sienna noticed that he seemed a bit crestfallen. The invites to the restaurant evening were mainly done by phone so there were swift replies. Everyone seemed very excited to be coming; Lily asked if she could bring her latest beau and Alphonse was now happy to pay for himself. Ernst was worried about finding a suitable restaurant as they were usually booked up well in advance at this time of year. He tried several well-known ones, unsuccessfully, then remembered 'Chez Etienne', just around the corner from Sienna's flat and tucked away in a small square. Etienne was an old and trusted friend of his father's and he welcomed Ernst warmly.

"I would be honoured to do the meal," Etienne said. "We don't get so booked up because we are so far off the beaten track and away from the tourists. We attract mainly French people who are regulars. I will prepare a menu for you to look at and you can decide on the food. The wine and other drinks can be decided on the night."
Sienna was delighted. She had so much to do before catching her plane home on the twenty-second. There were presents to be bought, an essay to finish and she had to replace her suitcase which had been damaged on her trip to Paris by over-enthusiastic luggage handlers. However, she felt energized and happy. Looking very much like a young lady in the first flush of love suited her well. Her step had the extra bounce that is common when in this state of mind! She ignored the heavy grey skies and damp, dismal weather; all was fine in her world.

A few days later there was a call from Etienne, to pop round soon with Ernst to discuss the menu and the seating arrangements. Ernst and Sienna spent a couple of days together walking arm in arm around the brightly coloured Christmas markets. The French seemed to use them as much as the stores to buy gifts. Sienna managed to find a few unusual treats to take back to England for her family. Back at the flat they laughed and cuddled over yet more hot chocolate, they made love and they even talked about the future. By now Ernst was spending several nights a week at Sienna's flat and they felt closer than ever.

It was soon time to go to Etienne's restaurant to sort out the meal. Sienna approached the deep red-brick-coloured building not knowing what to expect. She had rarely eaten out at home, let alone in Paris, as it seemed all a bit too expensive for her student budget. As they entered and were greeted by Etienne, she took in her surroundings and was not disappointed. The room was warm and welcoming with the cosy flickering flame of a real log fire. It had a very convivial atmosphere. The clientele had not yet arrived, so they sat down at a table and as Ernst chatted with Etienne at an incomprehensible pace, Sienna looked around her.

The mood seemed pleasantly casual. Individual dark wooden tables – some round and others oblong – were placed at regular intervals around the room and covered with red checked tablecloths. There were matching wooden chairs with plump, red cushions. On the floor was a subdued ochre-coloured carpet, with a small dark brown check pattern. The walls were covered with posters and pictures of Paris and framed in the same warm dark brown as the tables. Various lamps with white cloth and draping shades, some of which were fringed, lit up the room discreetly. At the bar area, propped up against a wooden post, was a large blackboard where Etienne or Sylvie – his wife – wrote the day's fare. Next to that on the bar stood a bronze statuette and an old-fashioned enamel pot with a tall cactus in it. At one end of the bar there was an upright square of decorative antique glass, which seemed to have no particular purpose than to add to the creativity of the room. The tables were laid out with gleaming, delicate, large wine glasses, carved salt and pepper mills and folded, luxurious linen napkins. Ernst chatted about the menu animatedly and agreed to ask the guests which options they would prefer for some of the courses. She heard Ernst tell Etienne that some subtle background music would be good.

"But," Ernst was adding, quite strictly, "absolutely no Jazz!" Sienna was very surprised at this – *weren't they all Jazz-lovers who were coming?*

"Please, *Chérie*, just leave it to me," said Ernst, kissing her forehead tenderly. They left, happy that it was all arranged.

The evening finally arrived, and Sienna was alone at home, getting ready. Ernst would arrive soon. She had her hair coiffed and wore it up on her head with a few loose tendrils dancing on her cheeks. She was wearing an exquisite lingerie set by La Perla that she'd just bought, along with her new black dress which she put on, excitedly. It was sleeveless and tight-fitting. *Hmm, I actually look quite sexy!* She murmured to herself, having had the usual hang-ups that girls her age often had, for several years. She put on some dangly silver earrings and natural-looking make-up. The doorbell rang and there stood Ernst looking extremely handsome in a black velvet jacket and pristine white shirt, his trousers were grey with a sharp crease and his shoes shiny black patent and pointed. As Sienna bent over to kiss his cheek, she could smell the aroma of his heady after-shave which he always wore, and it awoke her senses - every time.

"Entre Ernst! *Que tu es beau ce soir!*" ("Come in, Ernst, how handsome you look tonight!")

"And you, my darling, look sensational!" As he sat down he looked her up and down and said, "But Sienna, there is something missing..."

"Oh, my *parfum*, yes," and she went to get it.

"No Sienna, you have a bare neck." He produced a little black velvet box, tied with a large, silvery chiffon bow.

"May I?" he asked, and upon opening the box he revealed a delicate and unusual silver choker which he carefully draped around her neck. "It's an early Christmas gift, darling, as we won't be together."

It was a stylish and thoughtful gift, Sienna thought, which sat delicately around her neck and added perfectly to the elegance of her dress. She was beginning to feel so much love for Ernst and his caring nature was something she had yet to meet in a man, save her own father, who doted on her – as father's do. A niggling feeling inside questioned how things would turn out, though. She was, after all, only in Paris until August.

Chapter Eighteen

At long last it was time for the restaurant soirée. Sienna threw a white cashmere wrap over her shoulders and set off hand-in-hand with Ernst, walking in the fresh night air. Nobody else had yet arrived so they had time to check out the place settings and choose the wine. Sienna loved it there. She found Etienne so friendly and amusing and she also liked his plump little wife, Sylvie, who usually brought the meals to the tables whilst Etienne cooked. Alphonse arrived first with Mireille and Theo. As they entered, all smiles, Sienna was delighted to see that everyone had made an effort to dress up for the occasion. Alphonse was wearing an immaculately-ironed cream-coloured shirt (showing that he did, in fact, actually own an iron!). Over this was a vibrant, rust coloured waistcoat. His trousers had neat creases and for once he didn't wear 'those boots'; they were replaced by smart tan lace-ups with a pattern of small graduated holes on the toes. *He actually looks quite snazzy!* thought Sienna. Theo followed Alphonse, looking rather flamboyant. He wore a striking embroidered silk jacket, the colour of demerara sugar. Sienna noticed his beautifully manicured nails with a smile. His ponytail was now twisted into a neat bun, and Sienna could have sworn she saw a trace of mascara on his sweeping lashes. On his feet sat aubergine leather mules, teamed with grey silky-looking chino-style trousers with turn-ups. Mireille held his arm daintily. She looked delectable, as usual, in a lightweight Yves St Laurent trouser suit, however Sienna noticed that she looked especially delicate and pale, if not a little frail, that evening.

    The next couple to make an entrance was the wonderfully chic Lily, on the arm of her beau, Emile. Lily walked in gracefully, looking stunning as usual, and incredibly svelte, her arm threaded through Emile's. It seemed rather strange to see her without Fifi pulling behind her, but she was happily clutching this tall – rather dashing – young man, who was dressed in an impeccably-tailored charcoal suit, teamed with a light grey silk shirt worn open at the neck. An eye-catching couple, if there ever was one. Lily's dress was Japanese style, tailored from a black satin-like fabric with a high mandarin collar – very much in vogue at that moment. Here and there tasteful delicate sprigs and clusters of flowers were embroidered on the fabric, mimicking the traditional Japanese look. She wore shiny, see-through, natural-coloured stockings on her long legs which seemed to reach up to the Heavens. Her dainty shoes were black and incredibly high and sleek. Lily clasped a tiny, beaded pink clutch bag in one hand and with the other she held onto Emile, smiling broadly. Sienna held her breath as she admired her beauty, knowing that she could never reach such *Parisian Perfection*. The best thing about Lily, though, was her loving personality; Sienna absolutely adored her.

Xavier rushed in next, exclaiming that he was sorry he was a tad late, but that Paris traffic was appalling that evening. He was, of course, being Xavier, well-dressed in a navy suit and striped shirt with matching tie, which was tied loosely in a casual manner and not tight around his neck. He had given a lift to Freya, who had been delighted to accept his offer. Xavier was an attractive man and Freya found his company enchanting. She had beamed when he complimented her on how she looked. Freya made quite an entrance. Ever the bohemian, she more or less floated in, in an unusual, long, frilled turquoise dress and flat, pink strappy sandals with tiny fringes at the top of the shoe. Her hair fell in loose ringlets and she wore an incredible amount of boho jewellery, some of which looked quite tribal, in wooden, abstract designs and shapes. A long, wooden pendant with a grey metallic circle at one end hung loosely from her neck which was almost covered by a long strand of small wooden beads. On one arm she wore a host of bangles in varying sizes and colours, reaching halfway along her arm. Freya looked radiant and was laughing a great deal all evening. Her charms were not lost on Xavier, who decided that Freya really was quite a sexy lady. He loved her easy, natural style and the way she tossed her hair. Xavier embraced Sienna, and said they should meet up soon, taking his seat near Freya.

The other guests – the barman, Sienna's friends from the Sorbonne – did not turn up. Ernst had a call from them to say they had come down with the seasonal flu bug. Sienna welcomed the pair whom she'd met at the Jazz Club and called 'the odd couple' to herself. She remembered that they were called Hélène and Henri and had been invited by Theo to the club. Sienna recalled meeting Henri at the Jazz Club when Hélène was draped over him. Henri had given the impression that he was a tad tipsy then. Sienna noted that he still gave her that impression, but was still eagerly sipping aperitifs, nonetheless.

Looking around her she felt that people were in a jolly mood, and the fact that they all knew each other added to the enjoyment of the occasion. She almost wished she wasn't going home for Christmas, but she knew it would be good to see her parents. She would miss Paris though. Ernst and Sienna sat in the centre of the room with Lily and Emile and Alphonse. The atmosphere was animated as everyone took their seats, chatting away merrily. Etienne had put on soft, suitable background music. Sienna looked across at Ernst as they chatted: he seemed relaxed and happy. Finally, the food was ready. Sylvie appeared with the first course – some people had elected to have pâté de foie gras on toast, others chose oysters.

"Sienna," Ernst pointed out, "the food choice is very seasonal. It's dishes we eat at Christmas, especially, here in Paris." Sienna sipped a light, white wine from the huge round glass and commented on the good choice. The room was full of Parisian small-talk: What films had everyone seen, what was shown at the Art Gallery this week, the state of politics in France and personal recommendations of books. Sienna noted *nobody* seemed to mention the grim weather, as undoubtedly would have been mentioned in England at every opportunity.

The *plat principal* (main course) followed, eventually with more bottles of full-bodied red wine. Sylvie was assisted by Etienne here and there as the steaming hot food arrived.

"Que c'est bon!" Alphonse exclaimed. "Etienne, you are an excellent cook!" The next course was *le Cerf* (Venison) which had been cooked to perfection and served with seasonal vegetables – all arranged appetisingly in individual dishes. By now everyone was really relaxed, and Lily and Emile were even dancing slowly in a corner to the slow, melodious tracks that Etienne played. Quite suddenly, out of the blue, Ernst summoned Etienne and said to him firmly, "Etienne, my brother, I did tell you NOT to play Jazz!" Erroneously there had been one track included in the music that was a Jazz song – and a well-loved one. Ernst seemed inexplicably angry about this. Sienna looked very puzzled as Etienne went to change the music immediately. Lily and Etienne were dancing. Alphonse looked down at his feet.

"Whatever is wrong, Ernst?" asked Sienna, in surprise.

"Sienna, *ma Chérie*, you don't need to know. It's all settled, so let's enjoy ourselves, eh?"

Sienna thought best to ignore it and carried on laughing and enjoying the company and the excellent food. Just then Etienne returned to tell them that Mireille was feeling unwell and having a panic attack. Lily went to her at once and took her outside for some air.

"Mireille," she said gently, "maybe you shouldn't have come. Would you like me to call a taxi to take you home?"

"No, no," said Mireille "It was just..."

"I understand." Lily said. "Are you going to be okay now?"

Mireille had a walk outside and then sat quietly with a glass of water before returning to her table. Etienne came over to her and asked if he could get her anything and recommended she join in with the others for the Christmas Dessert – the *Bûche De Noël* (Christmas log).

This was a French tradition and all the patisseries tried to make the best Bûche at Christmas time. It was absolutely delicious, and the atmosphere returned to normal. They then had coffee, as Ernst and Sienna had decided they would not all go back to her flat as they atmosphere was so convivial, and Etienne and Sylvie were showered with compliments about the evening. At around two o'clock people started to say their goodbyes, leaving Ernst and Sienna to say their thanks to Etienne and Sylvie and walked back to her flat, hand-in-hand.

"Thank you so much for arranging it, *Chérie!*"
Ernst hesitated.

"Sienna, please don't be offended but I would like to go back to my flat tonight, is that okay?"

"Are you unwell, Ernst?" she asked. "My darling, what's wrong? Have I upset you unknowingly?"

"No, of course not, Sienna. It's just me, I have dark moods, sometimes. You'll see, I'll be right as rain tomorrow!" and with that, he kissed her goodnight and disappeared off in his little car. Sienna was baffled, but nevertheless slept well. The red wine had left her a little dizzy at first but then she entered a deep, peaceful sleep. When she finally awoke, she felt a bit cross with Ernst, for just leaving with no good reason. She was normally placid and very affable but occasionally she felt that people 'put on her' as she was so accommodating.

Why should I have to put up with black moods? she thought.

Chapter Nineteen

"Xavier! It's Sienna, here," she had picked up the phone in the afternoon after a long, lazy day, sleeping and reading. "Can we meet up? Tomorrow – lunch? That will be fine. Les Deux Magots?" Wow, that's a treat and it's on you for Christmas? Thanks so much, Xavier! And see you then at midday!"

Sienna hadn't seen or spoken to Ernst that day yet, but she thought she would give him some space. This seemed to work admirably, as the phone rang the following day before she went to meet Xavier.

"Sienna, I'm so sorry, but sometimes I just need to be alone. Can we put that behind us and do something tomorrow? I have to pop over to Milly today as *Maman* has a problem with her guttering and her odd-job man is ill. So, you're meeting Xavier? That's great – speak again tonight – or tomorrow morning?"

Sienna felt pleased to have spoken to Ernst and set off happily to meet Xavier the next day. They embraced like long lost friends and were soon chatting away nineteen to the dozen. Being with Xavier was so comfortable, just as always, like having a brother to share things with. They ordered a delicious lunch, which included a *croque monsieur*, which was ham and melted cheese on toast, a firm favourite of Sienna's.

"Xavier... I need to talk to you about Ernst." Xavier had thought this might happen, so he was prepared.

"I love him so much," Sienna continued, "but he's acting so strangely." She proceeded to tell Xavier about him not liking the Jazz music at the restaurant and then skulking off home afterwards.

"Sienna..." Xavier said tenderly, taking her hand. "That, I'm afraid, is Ernst. He's a lovely man, but he's very complex and sometimes very sensitive. He has dark moods, where he just needs to be alone until they pass."

"But I think I must have done something wrong, Xavier..."

"No, no, Sienna. It's just the way he is. I think it's hard for him – he has his asthma and he was very close to his father, who died suddenly a few years ago."

"He won't talk to me about him, Xavier."

"People grieve in very different ways, Sienna. If I was you, I would try and love and support him through his moods. It won't be easy, of course, but it's depression – he's not cross with you. You have been the best thing that could have happened to Ernst, Sienna, and I'm sure he loves you. After all, we all have our own foibles. I'm sure you have some too – like me?!"

"Well, yes," Sienna admitted. "I'm sometimes not that great first thing in the morning, until I've completely woken up with a couple of coffees!"

"And for me," Xavier laughed "I get annoyed with people who expect long phone calls and never seem to get to the point. It drives me mad! So, you see…"

Sienna felt a lot better and thanked Xavier. I'm going to try really hard to make Ernst happy, but give him the space he needs sometimes. She trusted Xavier's opinions – he seemed to have an old head on young shoulders. They chatted about all sorts of things, catching up on what they had been doing. Xavier asked for the bill and Sienna thanked him for a lovely Christmas present. Xavier asked if she was free that afternoon and, if she was, suggested he might show Sienna the Rue Mouffetard, which was only a stones-throw away.

"It's a famous and historical street market, with lots of wonderful produce and food, little shops, bars and bistros. Would you like to have a look around?"

Sienna nodded enthusiastically, as she hadn't yet been there and was always eager to see more of Paris, especially on the Left Bank, which she adored.

Xavier got up when they had finished, to take Sienna to a new location, that he knew she would love. It was only a short walk to the Rue Mouffetard. Sienna was enthralled by what she saw! A feast for the eyes lay in front of her. Xavier smiled.

"Ah, yes, here you find every sense is awakened – by amazing sights, sounds and smells. Enjoy, Sienna!" The Rue Mouffetard, Xavier explained, was a busy, bustling neighbourhood and one of Paris's liveliest ones. Sienna could already sense the feeling of old Paris here as they walked along the narrow, cobbled street, admiring the stalls and old houses along with all the colourful produce. There was so much to choose from; and the produce was carefully arranged on the stalls by the proud owners.

"Oh, I see, Xavier! It's a food market!"

"Well, mainly, yes."

Colourful vegetables and fruits were so nicely displayed, cheeses, sausages, chocolate, roasting chicken and other meats and fish were all temptingly lined up on the stalls. It felt like a truly French experience to Sienna, with its special charm and laid-back atmosphere.

"Mmm..." murmured Sienna, "these sights and smells are mouth-watering, it's all so quaint, Xavier." As they walked along the sound of music echoed from one end which added to the enjoyment and Sienna noticed that some people were dancing, too, in folk costumes. They passed numerous bistros, crêperies and brasseries and she noticed a wine shop, a honey shop and a shop selling olive oil as they moved along the crowded street. There were a few stalls selling what looked like real antiques that didn't cost a fortune and they stopped to admire them.

"Xavier, Sienna!" A lady in a long, striped dress rushed from one of the stalls. It was Freya! They embraced each other with surprise.

"I'm just selling a few things off at good prices here today..." Freya told them. "Can I interest you?" she asked, with a twinkle in her eye.

"Not today, Freya but great to see you!" Sienna spoke for both of them. "But I shall be coming to see you at your shop soon and I might be tempted. I need to come and see what Ernst sells and see his shop. That visit is overdue!" They left Freya serving an old lady in black who was hunched over a small lamp she had taken a fancy to. She was clutching a rather tattered little black leather purse, as though it contained the Crown Jewels. She wanted that lamp desperately, but clearly couldn't afford it. True to her kind nature, Freya wrapped it up quickly but securely and gave it to her. The old lady bustled off calling "God bless you!" to Freya in a somewhat croaky – but grateful - voice. Xavier looked at Freya with admiration. Sienna had wanted to ask Xavier how he was nowadays, so the next port of call was a coffee house which emanated the tempting smell of strong coffee along the street.

"Are you still missing Gabrielle much, Xavier?"

"Well yes, I must confess I do miss her, but it's getting more bearable. I have accepted it totally and I'm looking forward to Spring, when I can travel with my job. *Les affaires du coeur*, eh?" ("affairs of the heart?") he said, wryly. "They never run smoothly."

Sienna nodded in agreement but had decided to forget the other evening when Ernst disappeared off home.

"Thank you, Xavier," she said as they parted company and embraced each other. "You are a dear friend and a very special person. Will see you after Christmas, eh?"

Chapter Twenty

Sienna sat munching her croissants and thinking about her life. She'd only been in Paris a few months but so much seemed to have happened and so unexpectedly. She'd met some amazing people and seen a lot of the city she had grown to love. She'd rekindled her love for Jazz and met a gorgeous Frenchman who she loved. What's not to like? Sadly, her studies had not gone to plan. She tolerated her lectures and bluffed her way shyly through tutorials on things she either hadn't bothered to read on or had no interest in at all. She wondered – *where was all this leading? When I came here,* she ruminated, *the idea was to get a good qualification and then return to the UK and either teach in adult education or become a translator. Translation appeals... but why am I ploughing my way through countless French 'Treasures of Literature' with such a heavy heart?* Who were her real friends? Well, she was closest to Ernst, of course, but also very close to Lily, and Xavier, and then there was Freya and Alphonse. Xavier is an extraordinary man and such a dear friend. He has the ability and intuition to sum up people and situations and impart his wisdom as to how they should be handled. Sienna sometimes thought he could actually see *inside* her. Sometimes she would start a sentence and he would finish it – perhaps they were twins in another life? She hoped that his wanderlust didn't mean he would never find anyone to settle down with, as he was a man with much to give. She remembered her early days in Paris when she had felt unsure, insecure and sometimes homesick. Xavier knew just where to take her to cheer her up and when and how to make her laugh again. She smiled as she remembered. Then there was Lily; a darling of a friend. She understood Sienna. She would cleverly guide her through the pitfalls of being a young woman 'alone' in a big, cosmopolitan city.

Sienna had no idea that her life was about to change. When she awoke, she felt strangely expectant. She didn't quite know why, but she knew that pondering about her life the day before was nudging at something deep inside her — a feeling of being totally unfulfilled... *yes, that's what it was!* Whatever she was doing here in Paris, attending lectures that didn't interest her and enjoying her life there so much and yet she sensed a deep emptiness that needed addressing. She got ready to go out, putting on her casual, newly-found Parisian clothes. She zipped up her cosy, grey, suede coat and matching grey suede boots and grabbed her huge pink woollen scarf and almost ran out of her flat. Today, she was off to see Ernst's flat and his shop — at long last — and would see her wonderful man again and where he hung out. After yet another walk through the now-familiar cobbled streets, shiny and mottled by the morning rain, she arrived at Ernst's shop.

Ernst was the owner of a quite a large, old, grey-brick building which oozed character and which he had bought with money his father had left him. On the ground floor was a spacious shop area, with a small doorway which led into the room Freya sold her *objets trouvés* from. She rented the room from Ernst and loved her job. A twisting, aged, wrought-iron spiral staircase led up to two apartments. To the left was Freya's and to the right was Ernst's.

"Sienna, *ma Chérie!* I've missed you so much!" Ernst enveloped her in his arms and squeezed her tightly.

"How are you today, Ernst?" Sienna enquired.

"Oh, I feel fine now, and it seems forever since I last saw you," he replied, tenderly, holding her soft face in his strong hands and covering it with little kisses.

"Come, Sienna. Have a look at where I work and live."

He showed Sienna around the intriguing, rather dusty little shop, which displayed all the nooks and crannies and old-world charm of a Parisian building of former years. It's bare brick walls and marked stone floor — scattered with various ethnic rugs — lent to its general appeal. Ernst sold antiques: true antique furniture and some smaller items of value, not the bric-a-brac that Freya found at her markets which were scattered far and wide. These were high quality Parisian antiques and pieces from old Parisian dwellings or - occasionally – Châteaux, that people brought to Ernst. He was respected in his trade and either bought from them and resold the items or sold on their behalf, taking a generous commission for his efforts. Either way, the shop had been doing well for a number of years. Ernst had originally bought it from a Monsieur Bertrand, a well-known Parisian antique dealer who had retired to Nice. Sienna found it intriguing; she loved antiques and spent some time wandering around, admiring the mostly dark-coloured and often highly-polished furniture of a bygone age. After that, she followed Ernst up the beautiful iron staircase to his flat above.

"Wow!" Sienna exclaimed. It was truly stunning. She'd always known that Ernst was a man of taste. The floor was of deeply polished wood, darkened by age and two long, highly patterned Persian Kilim rugs lay between a couple of muted green sofas. These were piled with a mound of ethnic cushions in all colours of the rainbow but arranged so that the colours didn't clash. There was a central chandelier-like light fitting in bronze which gave out a low, dusky and dim light. This was amplified by the light of two old bronze lamps and a host of large, deep-orange candles – all lit. An old fireplace had crackling logs already ablaze and two tall floor candles stood on either side, flickering their subtle, warm candlelight into the room. Two dark wooden sideboards stood along one wall and housed wooden bowls, piled high with seasonal fruits and some exotic ones from abroad. A couple of dark wrought-iron side tables were next to the sofas and housed metal ashtrays, magazines and piles of books. Sienna picked up a book as Ernst prepared some lunch. It was Hemmingway's *A Moveable Feast* about his time in Paris: she immediately wanted to borrow it.

After lunch Ernst carried Sienna to the bedroom as he had done that first time they made love in Sienna's flat. This time they were more comfortable with each other and there was no timidity as they quickly removed each other's clothing, and kissed in an urgent, passionate way, moving their hands over the other's body until they could no longer wait...

"*Je t'aime, Sienna...*" breathed Ernst, as they made love on the soft cream bedspread and then lay breathless in each other's arms, Sienna flushed and smiling.

"Sienna, you have made me so happy," murmured Ernst. "I cannot live without you, my strong and sexy girl!" Sienna looked radiant as she fingered his tousled hair.

"And I, my Ernst, I want to stay in Paris forever...I love Paris so very much...and you."

When they finally dressed and cosied up in front of the crackling fire in the sitting room, Sienna announced, "Ernst, I have something I need to discuss with you. I can't go on with my studies a minute longer, I don't sleep for worrying about my next essay or tutorial. I hate what they teach me, and it has no relevance on my life. In a few days I'm going home and I'm going to announce to my parents that I'm quitting my studies. I don't know what they will say..."

"Well, Sienna, that's quite a bombshell! But you will be coming back to me after Christmas?"

"Oh, of course Ernst. I will be missing you. Fortunately, the rent on my apartment has been paid for another few months. It will be okay. I will probably have to come back and find a job." Ernst looked slightly pale: he feared she might not return.

"Don't be silly, Ernst! Everything will be fine, you'll see." Sienna spent the evening packing at home whilst Ernst was drinking Schnapps and worrying about Sienna not returning.

Chapter Twenty-One

Xavier pulled up outside Sienna's flat at eight o'clock in the morning. By coincidence he was dropping some tourists off at the airport in Paris and offered to take Sienna there. Ernst was unhappy – *he could have closed the shop and taken Sienna – why did she want Xavier to take her?* he ruminated. Sienna had laughed, "Only because he's going that way and it's convenient! Now stop this nonsense, Ernst! I'm only away for a few days, and then we will take up where we left off."

Begrudgingly, Ernst let the subject go and prepared for his visit to *Maman* in Milly-La-Forêt. He would talk to her about Xavier.

"Sienna spends too much time with him," he would tell her. "*Ce n'est pas normal, Maman, eh?*" ("It isn't normal, is it?")

Mr Stevenson collected his daughter from the airport in England and drove her back home to Norfolk. It felt so very strange. It was raining, of course, and it seemed eerily quiet. The pace was so slow after the bustle of Paris. Her mother was waiting with outstretched arms and gave her an enormous hug.

"Now, come in, my dear and sit down. Your dad will take your luggage upstairs, whilst I make a cup of tea."

And so the first of four days passed quite unremarkably with other family members and neighbours popping in. On Christmas Day, there was lots to eat and drink. Sienna's presents from Paris were much appreciated as they were, her mother remarked, 'rather different'. Boxing day was very quiet and apart from a few walks with the dog, Sienna felt a little bored. She missed Ernst, she missed her friends and most of all she missed Paris! It seemed like a good opportunity to broach *the* subject. Whilst they were relaxed with a drink in hand, that evening Sienna, gulping slightly nervously, made her announcement.

"Mum, Dad, I have something to tell you which you may not like. I'm quitting my studies in Paris."

"WHAT!" cried her dad. "This can't be true. We thought you seemed so happy?"

"Well, yes, I am happy with my life in Paris, but my studies hold no interest for me and are not what I expected." She went on to explain the nature of her lectures and how unhappy she felt. Her mother, who was a placid soul, asked tentatively, "Sienna, are you coming home? What are you going to do?"

"No, Mum...I'm afraid not. As you know, I have a boyfriend now, a wonderful circle of friends and, well, I've fallen in love with Paris."

"OK. I see we have to accept that, but what work or study will you do?"

Sienna sighed, as her father began to wring his hands.

"I'm so grateful for all of your support and especially for the flat. I guess now I will have to find a job and support myself. I don't know quite how as yet."

They talked it through for over an hour until her parents were satisfied that this was not a whim, and that it was really what she wanted to do. They loved Sienna, and, as an only child, they concentrated on her well-being as a priority.

Finally, her father said, "Well, Sienna, we have to respect your wishes and so I will be prepared to help you out financially until you are settled in a new job."

"Oh, Dad, thank you, thank you!" cried Sienna. She had always been especially close to her father and expected him to be agreeable when he had chewed the facts over. Mrs Stevenson nearly always went along with her husband and so she nodded agreeably. Sienna slept like a baby that night. She felt it was the beginning of a life with no restraints.

Chapter Twenty-Two

Ernst was waiting for her at the airport on her return and sighed with relief as he rushed towards her and took her suitcase. He kissed her gently on the cheek and gave a broad smile.

"Sienna, I've hated life without you here."

"Didn't you enjoy Christmas in Milly with your mother?"

"Oh yes, it was OK. You know, the usual round of relatives and endless conversations over very long meals about this and that."

"And have you been well, Ernst?"

"Not bad, Sienna. Christmas Eve was very busy and a very cold day, so I did have an asthma attack, but it wasn't severe as I was given several of *Maman's* special tisanes."

"Ernst, you do seem to have attacks when you are at Milly. I wonder why?"

"Just coincidence, I think, Sienna...let's get you settled into your flat and you can tell me what your parents have said about your decision."

Sienna cuddled up to Ernst and explained how everything had gone well, although they were rather surprised at what she had to say. Ernst enfolded her in his arms.

"My Sienna, don't worry about a thing. I will take care of you. Take a bit of time to decide what you are going to do."

They spent the rest of the afternoon listening to relaxing Jazz tracks from New Orleans, eating shortcake that Sienna had brought back from England and making tender - but passionate - love until it was beginning to get dark.

"Oh no! I have to be back in half an hour, my darling. I'm so annoyed. It's also rush hour traffic. I'm so sorry to go back this evening – I have a customer bringing over some particularly interesting pieces from an old Château that he wants me to look at…

He kissed her lovingly and hurriedly whilst getting dressed and dashed to the door. Sienna had forgiven him for rushing off the night of the restaurant. She'd listened to Xavier and she loved Ernst even more. Sienna sat contentedly, still listening to music and feeling optimistic. It had been a delicious afternoon with Ernst and now... well, this was going to be the beginning of the rest of her life – and the possibilities were endless!

Whatever was she going to do for a job? A temporary post of some sort would be good, she thought, *whilst she figured out what it was she really wanted to do.* First things first – tomorrow she had letters to write and appointments to make to see her professors and tutors at the Sorbonne. She thought about what she could do to make money, but drew a blank, so she decided to ring her close friend Lily and tell her the news.

"Sienna! Did you have a lovely time in England?" They exchanged stories about their Christmases. Lily had gone to Barbados with the lovely Emile and had a wonderful time in the sun. Sienna told her about her plans with trepidation, but again, all she got was encouragement.

"Sienna, you've been so unhappy with your studies, this is excellent news, and for Ernst too. Now I will put my thinking cap on and we must make plans with you. I believe you could be behind the bar at the Jazz Club for a while if you'd like, as one of the barmen is very ill and in hospital – they may never return. Not for you? Well...perhaps not, let me see! I know, I have it. You must teach children or adults English. Doing a language degree has given you a good grasp of grammar, *n'est-ce pas?*"

"But I have no qualification..." Sienna said.

"That doesn't matter, Sienna. I've known people do it. At least you will have a little money to supplement your parents' allowance. Right, I shall print off a little advert and display it in the Marais, in several places I know. I will also ask around for you. May I tell Xavier too as he has so many contacts? I can. Oh good."

Sienna's sleep was interrupted the next day by the phone.

"Sienna, *c'est* Xavier! I hope I'm not too early?" Rubbing her eyes, Sienna groaned.

"Yes, you are, Xavier. Yesterday was a long day and I planned to sleep in until late, but as it's you, I guess I'll cope..."

"Well, now that I know your new direction, I just had to tell you that I know of a client of mine who is going to England for six months and needs some tuition in English before he goes. Are you interested?"

"Absolument, Xavier! You're a star. Can you ring me later with the details? I'm so tired, I can't absorb much at the moment..." With that offer in mind, Sienna turned over again and nestled up under her thick and cosy winter duvet. A few minutes later, the phone rang.

"*C'est Ernst, Chérie. Ça va?*" Sienna loved hearing from him, of course, but clearly sleep was not on the cards this morning it seemed.

"I just rang to say how much I love you and how proud I am of you."

"That's sweet, Ernst." Sienna told him of Xavier's phone call and proposition.

"You've already spoken to Xavier then? Before breakfast too? Sienna, this is not on... you speak to Xavier all the time and he calls the shots. If he suggests you go to the Marais, you go and so on. Now he's finding you work?"

"Ernst, my darling, you're far too insecure. Xavier is like a brother to me!"

"A brother? Why do you need a brother when you have *me*?"

"I don't, Ernst, but we happen to get on so well and I met him almost as soon as I put my foot on Parisian soil..."

"It's not good enough, Sienna. You don't need him to show you around anymore, you have me, and any way he's given that job up."

"No – but we're good friends, that's all."

"How am I to know what's going on?" Ernst shouted angrily. Before Sienna had a chance to reply, he slammed the phone down.

"Uhhh!" grunted Sienna. "No sleep now..." she said, as she wearily put on her dressing gown and headed to the kitchen. After two cups of coffee, a croissant and half a brioche, Sienna decided that a long, serious conversation with Ernst had to take place. His moods and his asthma (although that wasn't his fault) were sometimes hard to handle, but this envy over Xavier which was escalating was becoming intolerable. She thought back to her other relationships. Although none had been really long-term, she had quite a few 'encounters' with the opposite sex.

She remembered Adrian at university: he had been desperately in love with her and she, very fond of him. It might have gone further but he was very insecure, so much so that he would often ring her number, withholding his own, just to see if she was really at home or out with someone else. Sometimes, he just wanted to hear her voice and he would ring her at night, when the answerphone was always on, just to hear her speak. She knew it was him, of course, and it woke her up, which was very annoying. They had a big confrontation where he had cried like a baby and promised he would never do it again. He kept his word, but the jealousy crept in in other ways and wore her down. It got so bad that he even resented her visiting her family as he was left alone, without her. One day she found him checking her opened mail, that lay on a table and she finished with him. Enough was enough. This was not going to happen ever again. Sienna was now very much her own woman, but she wanted to be with Ernst. She could see that he had unresolved issues, including very low self-esteem. Someone had once told her, "You can never truly love someone else, until you love yourself." And she had believed them.

"*Quelle horreur!*" she shouted out loud. The parrot she had inherited from the previous tenant said, "*Horreur!*"

She rang Alphonse, who was a wise soul. "Alphonse, can I come over today? I need to have a chat..."

Alphonse was only too pleased to have a bit of company, as painting alone in his studio could be very isolating.

Chapter Twenty-Three

Within a short time, tired as she was from the day before, Sienna had arrived at Alphonse's atelier. He greeted her with a huge bear hug and ushered her in.

"What's wrong, Sienna? Would you like a coffee?" He knew her well enough to know she wasn't happy. Sienna usually smiled, and people would comment on her lovely smile. Today it was missing: she looked glum. She sat down on the comfy sofa, having moved quite a few tins and boxes (presumably of paints) and piles of paper. She looked unhappily at Alphonse who was sitting opposite, a Gauloise hanging nonchalantly from his mouth and a coffee in his paint-splattered hand.

"Well..." Sienna began, "It's Ernst. He's stifling me, Alphonse. He always wants to be around me and when I see Xavier, he's jealous. That's getting worse, he's like a contender to the throne!"

"Ahh..." said Alphonse, pausing before he spoke "*La jalousie! C'est impossible.* Alas!" ("Jealousy. It's impossible!") Listen to me, Sienna. It isn't going to change easily – with jealousy, you can only temper it. We all have foibles, you know, but some worse than others." She thought quietly. "Oh yes, mine is frogs – I can't stand them."

"Well no, Sienna, that isn't exactly a foible, that's more of a phobia. A foible is a weakness in your character and sadly we have to try and tolerate each other's little foibles."

"But Alphonse, this isn't *little*. It's going to ruin our relationship..."

"Then you must talk with Ernst, as soon as possible. Communication is a priority in any good relationship, *n'est-ce-pas?*"

Sienna reflected and then said slowly, "Life is so much easier when you aren't involved in too much emotional stuff. It's like opening a can of worms. It makes me feel very vulnerable."

"Ah, *oui*, Sienna, but people are our life – our family, our friends, our lovers." Alphonse smiled, and Sienna suddenly felt very young and innocent.

"Suddenly all of this gallivanting around Paris feels a bit trivial, although I love it. The real stuff is in relationships, isn't it, Alphonse?"

"We learn from history and other people and you must continue to enjoy Paris and its history. It has so much to offer the soul. Your trips will be a welcome distraction and Xavier will still be able to take you when Ernst is not free."

"But that's just the problem, Alphonse. Xavier! Ernst is so jealous of him and whilst I regard him as the brother I never had, he won't listen."

"We all have problems to deal with Sienna. It's whether our foibles and problems can sit alongside the other person's successfully! I'm not unsympathetic, though, Sienna, ma Chérie. It's possibly some deep insecurity from Ernst's childhood. I don't know. You must find ways to distract your thoughts, Sienna. We are what we think, you know!"

Sienna hadn't really analysed her thoughts – or much else for that matter.

"If we think negative thoughts, then it leads to negative feelings and we can feel sad, depressed or anxious. Try to catch yourself doing it and change that thought to something positive. Distract yourself! Why do you think I paint? Yes, it's because God has given me a gift, but it's also an outlet for my emotions and they are often very negative ones, I'm afraid. We are all vulnerable."

Sienna watched and listened intently.

"But how? How do you know all of this, Alphonse?"

"My dear girl, it's life experience that comes with age!"

"You are a very wise man, but not so old!" Sienna laughed.

This was all a new way of thinking to Sienna, who rarely thought analytically about anything, although she noticed that Ernst did. She hadn't seen her friends as 'cardboard cut-outs'. She'd noticed some of their frailties, their strangeness and some of their mystery. Perhaps they had problems, too? She suddenly realised that she needed to get beneath the façades we all portray.

"Yes," replied Alphonse, when she told him what she was thinking. "We do all have masks and often we don't recognise them. Living in this beautiful city does not exclude problems, Sienna, romantic as it is!"

Sienna hugged Alphonse. "Thank you so much, my dear Alphonse. You've opened my eyes and I will try to be more understanding with Ernst and we will talk..."

It was tempting to postpone the tête-à-tête with Ernst and Sienna thought she would continue to let him "stew in his own juice" a while, whilst she spent the day relaxing at home. It was a bright but crisp day outside. For once, the sun had ventured from behind its screen of rather threatening, abstract-shaped clouds and a few weak rays streamed in through the window and gave promise to the dullness of her decor. Maybe she would take a stroll later. The book beside her looked inviting. Curious to know what it was like to live in the twenties in Paris – and spurred on by the twenties Jazz night, where she became acquainted with the music of the era – she'd purchased Hemingway's *A Moveable Feast* at last. She devoured his exquisite, precise narrative for a couple of hours. Sadly, her conscience then rebuked her for the chores she had left undone lately. She really should clear the cupboard in the corner of her bedroom which was full of clutter.

On arrival in Paris, she'd just dumped a lot of stuff haphazardly in here. She peered in at the piles of shoes, in all shapes and colours, well-thumbed books, an old sewing box, several large marked cardboard boxes which contained old photos, and a collection of well-tried recipes. It was impossible not to have a glance at the photos, some of which were in black and white and had been passed down from previous generations, often looking distinctly yellowed by now. She looked at the photos of her grandparents, of their parents and of various great-aunts and uncles that she didn't recognise. There was a photo of her parents' wedding. They didn't look much older than her and were clearly very happy. She wondered if that would ever be her. Her best find, however, was to come, when she came across her beloved box of watercolour paints. There were also a few brushes, now past their prime and with a few rather stiff, uneven tufts sticking out of their wooden handles, along with a collection of unsharpened pencils. She paused as she pictured herself at home, as a rather bored teenager, amusing herself by drawing the garden from the bay window at the back of the house. Sometimes in summer she would while away a few hours sitting on the freshly-mown lawn, under the laden apple tree, deftly sketching the rabbits in their tiny hutch. She could take her sketch indoors and paint until the paper was awash with colour and came to life. It had been a sad day when they no longer allowed her to pursue her beloved art at school and she was told to study Latin instead (*Useless language!*) in order to be able to do a French degree at University in the Midlands. Sienna had enjoyed her art lessons and was ecstatic when her work, quite often, had been pronounced the best in the class. Stopping herself abruptly from her reverie was a good idea, because thinking about home in any shape, could still bring on a nasty attack of homesickness, which was strange as it was not long since she had been home.

Chapter Twenty-Four

The phone rang: it was Ernst. He wanted to apologise; he didn't know what had come over him. He asked her if they could start again. He loved Sienna *á la folie* (madly) and could not envisage life without her.

"Ernst," sighed Sienna. "I love you too, but we do need to talk. If you wish you could come over this evening."

At eight o'clock, the doorbell rang. He stood there, head down, looking sheepish and bearing a striking bouquet of flowers he had picked from the flower market – the first of the pristine white spring blooms. Sienna hugged him and felt so relieved to see him again. He looked, somehow, rather fragile all of a sudden. She made a drink and Ernst, lowering his eyes, began to talk.

"Look, Sienna, I do know really that there's nothing going on between you and Xavier, but sometimes I just can't help myself. I get really black moods and I regret what I say..."

"Have you always been this way, Ernst?"

"Yes, I have but it was made worse by my father's death, and I feel responsible for *Maman* too. I was always insecure as a child, though. I think it's because...oh, I'm not sure..."

"Go on..." Sienna said, stroking his arm, gently.

"You see, my father whom I loved dearly wasn't my real father. My mother had an affair with a German man and I was the result. I was named Ernst after his father. He left before I was born and *Maman* went on to marry Pascal... and now he has gone too. Maybe I blame myself for my real father's departure. I'm not sure."

"Well, my darling, that's certainly a possibility. I know that when there is a separation or divorce, children often blame themselves..."

"You're so perceptive for your age, Sienna! Maybe that's why I'm insecure then. I know I'm complex. Do you understand me a bit better? I don't know if that explains my black moods though, but I promise to try hard not to be jealous and to give you the space you need. You are so precious, you know, so very precious..."

Sienna smiled. He knew everything was forgiven and he folded his arms gently around her and held her with a tenderness she hadn't experienced before. He'd said he loved her on many occasions, but this was the first time it really rang true. There was a sincerity and honesty in their lovemaking that - mingled with the passion – took Sienna's breath away. He stayed with her until Paris awoke them with the buzz of traffic, the trains from Montparnasse and the general hubbub of life.

"I must go. So sorry darling..." Ernst pulled away. "I have to be back at the shop to see a stall-holder with goods for Freya. She's away in Brittany hunting for interesting items to sell and not back until tonight."

Sienna smiled and her rosy cheeks, still flushed from their tender lovemaking, showed off the deep dimple in her cheek. She sat quietly for a while thinking about her life. The excitement of a new life without essays and lectures was beginning to rise within her. She could feel the sweet call of freedom at long last; freedom to do whatever she wanted and be whoever she wanted. Surely everyone deserves that?

The day outside looked crisp, but bright and brought promise that Spring was just around the corner. Small flowers were just about to burst into bloom in the sidewalks and some had already lifted their heads above the still-hard soil, offering new hope and a new beginning.

That's it! Sienna smiled to herself. *That's what I'm sensing. A new beginning for everything in my life...* She decided to go off exploring on her own, staying on this side of the city. Knowing that it was a cliché, and well-documented, she still believed that a wander through the streets here fulfilled romantic dreams. Deciding to start at Notre Dame, she leisurely crossed the bridge and found an abundance of booksellers or *bouquinistes* and artists selling prints. There were stamp sellers, and book vendors, who had set up along the embankment. A couple of braver artists had put up an easel and were painting, still muffled in jackets and scarves, despite the sunshine. She half-expected to see Alphonse. She stopped at several *bouquinistes* and had a browse through their used and antiquarian books, from their green- painted book stalls. It seemed to be a quintessentially Parisian pastime – and Sienna loved it. There must have been around two hundred stalls which seemed to combine books and antiques in such a picturesque setting. She was overwhelmed by the number of magazines, vintage finds and souvenirs as well as aged books. These *bouquinistes* were actually part of Paris' literary history, apparently, and her map told her you could find them from the *Quai de la Tournelle* to the *Quai Voltaire*. At one, she found a copy of Antoine De Saint-Exupéry's *Le Petit Prince* which she bought for Freya to give to one of the children, who always seemed to be in tow, and who had no books at all. She ended up chatting to the *bouquiniste*, who complimented her on her French and was explaining the heritage they had and how they had to adhere to regulations like the green paint on the stalls. The Parisians were not happy about the sale of souvenirs – but it was necessary.

Sienna wandered back through the well-trodden cobbled streets again, stopping for a coffee at a little corner café along the way. As she sat, contentedly sipping her drink, she felt a hand on her shoulder.

"*Bonjour! Ça va?*" a deep-ish voice exclaimed. She turned around but did not recognise the rather exotically dressed lady in front of her.

"Ah, you don't recognise me!" the lady said, pulling off a woollen hat to reveal a long plait. It was the Peruvian lady from the Jazz Club whose name escaped her, embarrassingly. She looked just like she belongs to one of the new groups of South Americans who played pan-pipes in the city centres at home, Sienna mused.

"I'm Hélène! I came to your Christmas dinner too, with my boyfriend Henri!"

"Yes, I remember you now! This Parisian air has numbed my brain cells *n'est-ce-pas*? Do sit down, Hélène, and have a coffee."

Sienna had no idea what to talk about with Hélène, but she needn't have worried, as her companion was a loquacious lady, who didn't pause for breath much between her sentences. They had a general chit-chat about the Jazz Club and Hélène told her that Henri was her boyfriend of eighteen months, but that she felt sure he wouldn't be in eighteen months' time due to his disturbing addiction to alcohol.

"I don't think he's an alcoholic, you know, Sienna. He just seems a bit tipsy most evenings," Sienna had noticed this but said nothing. "And you, my dear, I've seen you with Ernst. You make a lovely couple! I saw him the other day, deep in conversation with Xavier at a café in the Marais, although they didn't notice me. He seemed very agitated and as though he couldn't get his breath..."

"Yes, he has asthma," replied Sienna. "I must leave now. I'm sorry, Hélène, but I'm teaching English to a new student tonight..."

Making her way home and checking the time, Sienna felt very confused. *Xavier and Ernst? What ever could they be doing together...?* Although he promised not to be jealous again, Sienna had always had the impression that Xavier and Ernst would never be friends now. Hélène had also remarked that they were having an agitated discussion with much waving of arms and loud voices at one stage – but then that's a marker of the French, anyway. Sienna decided she could either confront Ernst about this *secret meeting* or let it lie and continue in their present bliss. She decided to do the latter... If Ernst was telling Xavier off for showing her too much attention, then it was his problem ...not hers!

Chapter Twenty-Five

The chug and rattling of Ernst's old car pulling up outside alerted Sienna to his arrival, early the next morning: that car definitely needed replacing. Sienna grabbed her coat, scarf and bag and ran out into the wintry sunshine. Ernst was waiting to take her to see the magnificent Château and gardens at Fontainebleau, just outside of Paris. He was eager to get away from the city bustle again, and the pollution that didn't help his lungs. The day was bright and promising, and the light air felt invigorating as she left the flat expectantly. After kissing Ernst on the cheek and briefly cuddling up close to him, she spied a few things on the back seat.

"What are the green bottles and little packets for, Ernst?"

"Oh, they are herbal things *Maman* needed and couldn't get hold of. Milly is only around twenty minutes from Fontainebleau, so I thought we could drop them in on the way, if that's okay?"

"Of course," Sienna replied, secretly pleased that she would see Madame LaFargue again; she was such an interesting lady.

After arriving in Fontainebleau after a leisurely drive through the countryside, they headed for the forest.

"I thought we could take a walk here, while the sun's still out," Ernst suggested. It was a really spectacular and rather 'different' forest. Sienna was glad she was wearing her well-worn but trusty walking boots. As well as the different trees, the vegetation and flora and fauna were special. They reached an area which had very unusual rocks of all shapes and sizes which seemed weirdly to look like different animals. According to the guidebook they had, these were actually naturally formed. As they walked on they both noted the incredible calmness and peace of her surroundings. The parkland and the gardens around the Château seemed very quiet too, a welcome change to the Parisian noise. They headed towards the Château, where the borders housed hundreds of daffodils which were just beginning to wake up from their winter sleep. As they walked along, arms entwined and the sunshine beating down on their happy faces, Sienna couldn't remember when she last felt so settled and carefree. It was a very special day. Paris felt like a million miles away as they walked along the gravel paths together, creating precious memories. They shared jokes, they laughed, talked about the music they both liked and even planned a skiing holiday in the Alps the next year.

As they approached the Château, they passed more and more borders of Spring flowers, ready to burst open and form a carpet of intermingling, vivid colours. *Ernst looks well, and happy*, thought Sienna. He wore a permanent smile that day and his teeth looked startlingly white against his olive complexion and dark lustrous hair. She'd never seen him look so relaxed and savoured the moment. The weather was changing again – as it frequently did in February – so they decided to just look at the outside of the Château before heading to Milly. It didn't disappoint and was every bit as sophisticated as other grand French Châteaux. It oozed 'old charm' and had been beautifully restored and maintained. The guidebook said it had been a hunting lodge once and that Napoleon had signed his abdication here, which interested Sienna. The quietness prevailed – apart from a few workmen and a small group of children. They set off for Milly, as the rain began to leave tiny, random splashes on the windscreen. Madame LaFargue opened the door and greeted them warmly. Sienna was surprised to see her looking a tad frail and she was stooping somewhat. Her rosy complexion was now rather pale and drawn.

"*Maman*, how are you?" Ernst enquired.

"Well, my son, I'm doing well but winter has taken its toll and I have to rest more now, I'm afraid." As she led them into the sitting room she seemed a little breathless. She had Ernst when she was a little older than most and was now in her sixties. "I guess I'm just getting a little older!" She laughed. Ernst gave her the bottles and packets of herbs and tincture for which she seemed very grateful.

"I'm so sorry but we can't stay this time. Sienna is teaching one of her new pupils tonight."

"Will you take tea with me before you go?" She was pleased when they sat in the cosy sitting room and caught up with the news. Sienna explained why she was teaching and that she had left her studies. Ernst reassured his mother that he was well, but that business was not good at the moment, then she retired to her room for a sleep and they went happily on their way back to Paris. *It has been a remarkably happy and relaxed day,* Sienna mused on their return and she thankfully removed her constricting boots, bade Ernst farewell and lay down on the sofa to listen to an English radio programme.

Chapter Twenty-Six

Sienna was awakened yet again by an early morning phone call. "Why do people do this?" She said out loud, grumpily.

"*Bonjour*, Sienna. It is Freya."

"Oh hello, Freya, I haven't spoken to you for a while. I was just thinking we must–"

"–Sienna," interrupted Freya, "it's Ernst. He collapsed earlier and could hardly breathe. It was so early he told me not to worry you. I got a taxi and took him to hospital."

"Oh no!" Sienna cried. "where is he now? Is he OK?"

"Yes, he's okay but still at the hospital."

"I will get a taxi and come immediately."

"Thank you, then I can get back to the shop and I will deal with Ernst's customers too."

The hospital was about thirty minutes ride away. Sienna felt anxious and did not know what to expect. She found Ernst, tucked up in bed on a small ward. He looked pale and exhausted; his eyes had lost their sparkle from the day before and his breathing seemed rather laboured. She kissed him gently on the forehead and asked what had happened.

"I don't really know. I was just gathering firewood together for the wood burner when I had a bad asthma attack. My inhaler was still in the car so by the time Freya found me I was in a bad way." A kindly looking gentleman in a white coat arrived on the scene as Ernst lay in the hospital ward.

"*Voilà*, Monsieur Colin!" the nurse introduced the respected specialist.

"Well, Ernst, how are you feeling now? You need to take a lot of rest when you get home, along with plenty of fresh air and absolutely no stress. I have prescribed some medication for you, but you know your lungs have been aggravated further by the smoke inhalation."

"Smoke inhalation? What smoke inhalation?" Sienna asked Ernst, as the specialist moved away on his round of the ward. Ernst looked away. "Oh that! It's nothing really, Sienna. It was a few years ago when I helped a friend trying to put out a bonfire which had escalated somewhat out of control. I'd forgotten about it."
Sienna wondered why he hadn't mentioned it, but let it go. The main thing was to get him home and look after him. A few hours later, after Ernst had a sleep and Sienna had wandered around the shops in the neighbourhood to pass time, she was able to collect Ernst, summon a taxi and take him home. She dutifully tucked him in bed and went to prepare some food on a tray. Ernst pushed it away, saying he wasn't hungry and needed to speak to Freya about the shop.

"Is that entirely necessary today, my darling?"
"Yes, just a quick word."

Freya came on the phone and assured Ernst she had taken care of the shop all day but sadly there had been no customers.

"Oh la-la, Freya..." he groaned. "What am I going to do? Business is terrible, and I owe so much money."

Sienna was surprised to hear this but told him they should talk and make a plan when he was better. Freya agreed to keep an eye on him overnight as he needed to rest alone in his own bed. She would bring him hot drinks and soup. Sienna kissed him gently again.

"I will be back in the morning, my love, but I order you to rest. Freya is here, and you can always ring me."

"What a strange day it's been," she said to the parrot as she got home. He didn't reply this time, perhaps because he sensed her sadness. Sienna returned every day in an effort to restore Ernst back to health. He was up and about by now, but had black moods, seemed depressed and looked generally frail. In fact, he seemed half the man he was. She looked after him when she wasn't teaching. She washed and ironed and cooked for him. It became more and more difficult to persuade him to go out.

"But I am happy here, Sienna! Why would I want to go out? Paris is polluted. It's cold and my asthma gets worse there." Sienna tried to reason with him that the Spring sunshine was on the way and short walks in places like the Jardin Du Luxembourg would make him stronger, to no avail. His body was stronger now, but his mood was so low that sometimes she would arrive during the day to find him huddled by the fire with the curtains closed. One day in particular she found him sobbing.

"Forgive me, Sienna, I've made a horrible mess of everything. You would be better off without me..." he cried.

"Don't be ridiculous, my darling. I love you the way you are, and you have made my life in Paris a wonderful experience." She stayed with him until evening. He ate very little and just had one glass of wine. She tucked him into his bed and said she would return tomorrow. It had been pointless staying overnight as Ernst slept fitfully and would often wander around at night or sit in a chair and read until he nodded off.

"Goodnight, my precious." She hugged him tight.

"*Au revoir*, my Sienna and thank you for looking after me."

The next day was rainy and windy and Sienna pulled her warm scarf across her face as she went to the local shops for food.

"*Bonjour Monsieur Martin*," she said, "I'd like some steak and pork with *un bon saucisson* to have at lunch time." Monsieur Martin smiled and nodded. He liked the English girl.

"And how is that boyfriend of yours now?" he asked with concern.

"He's still very low in mood and a bit frail. Thank you for asking, Monsieur."

Sienna walked to Ernst's flat. The rain had stopped, and she thought the air might invigorate her. Arriving at Ernst's place, Freya answered the door, looking upset and wiping away her tears. Sienna moved to go up to see Ernst.

"Don't go up," Freya said. "Sit down and let's talk..."

"No…No!" Sienna cried, fearing he had died, and ran upstairs. She pushed the old, weighty oak door open and could not believe what she saw. The bed was made, the curtains opened but no-one was there. Clearly Ernst had gone out. She went to his wardrobe and the antique chest of drawers: they were empty. Not only had Ernst disappeared, but all his possessions had gone, too. Everything. Sienna screamed in shock, "Freya...? Freya, where is he?"

Freya came up and put her arms around Sienna.

"I don't know, Sienna. I came up half an hour ago and this is what I found..."

"But didn't you hear him go out? You must have heard the car?"

"No, Sienna, I was at the *boulangerie*, getting baguettes and when I returned he had gone. The car is still there, parked at the back of the shop."

"What am I to do?" Sienna cried, as the hot tears poured down her flushed cheeks.

"I did find this letter though, on the table downstairs. It's for you. Let me make some hot chocolate for us and you open it." The large white envelope had *Sienna* written on it in black italics, which were running slightly down the page, belying the fact that someone had shed tears over the ink. Sienna shook all over as she read the letter.

My darling, Sienna, ma Chérie, mon amour,
You are and always will be the love of my life. I have loved every minute of every day and night we shared together. Time has showed me, however, that I am not the man for you. You deserve better. You need a strong, well and capable man who can look after you. Sadly, that's not me. My illness and my capacity to cope with it, along with my dark moods, have broken me. The business is not doing well at all and there will be no money for us to share our lives in the way you deserve. I've made mistakes in my life which haunt me every single day and are not part of "us".

So, my sweet girl, I want you to be strong and move on. Our friends will take care of you for now. I have gone away to try to start again – far away, where the warm climate will help my lungs, my depression and hopefully my mood swings. I know that you will do well. Carry on with your painting, whatever. Go to Alphonse for encouragement. He is a good man and brilliant artist, as you could be. Please pick up your paintbrush again. It will be an escape from your thoughts of me.

I have contacted Maman. She knows where I am but is sworn to secrecy. It is for the best. Maman owns the shop now and will sell it in due course.

Remember I will love you, Sienna, 'til my dying day.
Your Ernst xx

Sienna saw the tear stains on the paper and dissolved into loud sobs herself as she read the letter.

Chapter Twenty-Seven

Sienna turned pale and looked at Freya in disbelief.

"This can't be real, Freya!" she continued to sob violently, gasping for air.

"I'm as shocked as you, Sienna. He left a note for me, thanking me for everything. Telling me to look after you and about the sale of the shop."

"His mother will be heartbroken, Freya..."

"No doubt..." replied Freya, "but I know her. She is a tough woman and she may think it's for the best for his health. I don't know."

"But he hasn't even left me his address. Why not?" The pain was unbearable.

"Perhaps he doesn't want to prolong the hurt. I do know he loved you so very much. He clearly doesn't want contact, my poor Sienna. Maybe it will change in time..." Freya hugged her tightly.

"I've given up my studies, Freya, and was so looking forward to spending more time together."

"I am here for you, my dear Sienna, and I know Lily and all the others will be too. May I tell them?"

"Well, yes, I guess so..." Sienna was still crying uncontrollably. "You know, I really thought he was the one."

"I'm sure he thought you were too. I know Ernst well. He is intense – a complex character and his health gets him down – he is depressed. Come, I will walk home with you and make sure you have everything you need. I am there at the end of the phone, day or night."

Sienna was beginning to feel angry. "How dare he do this!" she cried out, as they walked home in the fine drizzle and biting February wind. "How could he?" she asked in rage.

At the flat, Sienna got under the duvet and cried uncontrollably.

"Silly boy! Silly boy!" The parrot repeated.

"Oh, go away! Shut up!" Sienna cursed at the creature. Her hair was wet with her tears, her eyes swollen and puffy as she stared at herself in the mirror. Only yesterday she had looked quite radiant. She got up and opened a bottle of Merlot, which she drank unashamedly until she slept.

The days and weeks that followed were torturous. Sienna stumbled around as if in a dream. She cancelled her English lessons for two whole weeks and shut herself away, only emerging to buy food at the local shops – most of which ended up in the bin as she had no appetite. The weight began to fall off her and she noticed she was losing strands of hair in the shower. The phone rang a lot. Lily had been the first to ring to try and comfort her. Dear Lily – then Alphonse, who asked her to visit him, but she declined. Freya rang every day and Xavier popped around with flowers, chocolates and wine.

"Sienna..." Xavier said, gently, with an arm around her shoulder. "As soon as you feel a little better, I shall take you out to a quiet restaurant, *d'accord*?"
Theo rang and quietly reassured her he was there for her. He spoke falteringly, not knowing what to say. Everyone had been so kind. Mireille was the last to ring, who surprisingly sneered at what Ernst had done.

"How dreadful of him, Sienna – but you know, that's Ernst for you." It hurt – but Sienna thought people were entitled to their opinions.

And so, the time passed. The days seemed to roll into each other, until one day Sienna awoke, looked out of the window and knew it was Spring at last. People were walking past with a bounce in their step and chatted more animatedly in the street. Paris, as everyone had always said, lent itself well to Spring. The grey, cloud-laden skies were suddenly replaced by the occasional smaller cloud, white and fluffy cotton-wool masses that floated in a blue expanse. Sienna didn't smile, but now had acquired an outer air of acceptance. She'd started to eat gradually, although not much more, and eventually decided to visit Alphonse. Inside she felt shaky, though. Taking her small, old box of paints and worn brushes with her, she arrived on his doorstep that morning.

"Alphonse, I've come to watch you work, if that's okay?" Alphonse welcomed her with open arms and a huge bear hug.

"*Ma Chérie*, I am so glad to see you are trying to move on from the heartache. Do come in. A drink and a fresh *tartine* maybe?"

Sienna sat down and replied hesitantly.

"It's still not easy, Alphonse. I had given my heart and now it feels like someone has plucked it from my body. It hurts... but no it's not quite as raw. I just feel lost now and I don't know what to do next." Sienna had a look at what Alphonse was painting. He was so talented. The paintings he was working on were light and luminous. One was abstract, another was of people walking in the rain along one of the boulevards. They both had a lightness of touch and the colours flowed into each other.

"Sienna, I see you have some watercolours? You should try. I will help you begin and you can gradually develop your talent. Would you like to sit here?" Alphonse pointed to a small easel nestling on a paint-splattered table. "You might find it easier and more comfortable to sit at first and gain some confidence. Are these your pencils to sketch with?" She nodded.

"*Mon Dieu*, Sienna!" he laughed, as he sharpened them all deftly with his knife. "Let's just do some sketching today? Here, use this eraser, there will be some mistakes which is normal." He positioned her by the window. "Now look out over the river and what do you see? You could maybe sketch the small boats over there, or if you prefer, the people admiring the souvenirs and prints at the *bouquinistes'* stalls? As you wish..."

Sienna could feel her body relaxing for the first time in weeks, as she sketched away happily for the very first time in years. She noted that the busier she was, the better, otherwise niggling thoughts of loss, rejection and the general heartache still weighed her down. At night she often woke up still and turned over expecting Ernst to be there. She resolved to do more art and make it a real hobby. Although in the "City of Art", she had neglected it since her arrival and pushed her pencils and paints to the back of the cupboard. Now she was feeling a sudden release. The blank page had invited her to be who she wanted to be, make any mark on it she cared to put and soon she had felt lost in her drawing. Two whole hours later, plus a tea-break, and it was finished.

"Sienna! That's beautiful! You have been hiding a gift. You must return and do more?"

"Oh, I'd love to, Alphonse," Sienna almost beamed, for the first time in months.

"But first of all, we must pay a visit to Theo. These pencils and paints are old and your brushes – well, they've seen better days!"

"*D'accord*, Alphonse!"

"I will ring you when I have another free day and we will go to the little art shop and sort you out..."

Sienna skipped back through the streets. It was the very first time she felt truly alive again. The sadness was there, but she'd pushed it down. The welcome sunshine had disappeared, but the promise of Spring still hung in the air and she noticed that the many tourists that were always in Saint Germain and the Latin Quarter had shed their dull, long overcoats, heavily padded jackets and woollen scarves for lighter jackets and pastel-coloured heavy sweaters and jeans. She thought about Fontainebleau and how beautiful the early Spring borders would look. She imagined the lambs frolicking in the green fields that they had passed through en-route. Her heart sank, and a single tear dripped onto her hand as she remembered the holiday they had planned, how he held her close, how his kiss felt. She opened her front door and rang to check her answerphone; there were no messages. He'd really gone forever.

Chapter Twenty-Eight

The next day was, well... just another day without Ernst. Today Xavier was picking her up at lunch time and taking her to a little bistro-type restaurant near the Opera. He said it was quiet, so they could talk. As she heard him pull up outside in his smart, white, shiny cabriolet, Sienna dashed down the concrete steps to the waiting car.

"Xavier!" They greeted each other with a kiss on each cheek. "I'm so pleased to see you again."
Xavier smiled and squeezed her hand. They had only managed to talk on the phone since the dreaded day she found Ernst had gone. Xavier had been abroad, inspecting hotels for his company and had just got back.

"Sienna, I don't know what to say, but when we are comfortably seated at the restaurant maybe I can help you with a few things. You know, my dear girl, I will always be available for you. I know I can't ever replace Ernst in your affections but if you want, I can take you out... there are still places you haven't seen in Paris yet, yes?"
She nodded. It was always comfortable with Xavier. *Just like old slippers,* she mused, *only better.* The bistro was almost empty, although usually very popular. It stood at the end of a quiet little side street in the Opera district. A few people were sitting outside reading newspapers or talking quietly. There was little noise. They decided to sit indoors, and Sienna was impressed by the unusual menu: it served Japanese food! Xavier knew that Sienna had wanted to try out Japanese fare, so she was impressed by his choice. The waiters were Japanese mainly but with some from Thailand. They all spoke fluent French, which seemed a tad incongruous when they opened their mouths. The tables had only chopsticks on them, but Xavier said he would show Sienna the skill of using them. The menu looked tasty, if not *different.* There were soup bowls full of white noodles, tempura (shrimp fried in batter), duck and tofu, as well as many other Japanese delicacies. They made

their choice and sat back with a drink. Xavier raised his glass, "To Sienna!" he said.

"Xavier, there is so much I don't understand. Ernst and I were ecstatically happy and when we went to Fontainebleau, we were even planning holidays together."

"My dear Sienna," Xavier said quietly. "What I am about to tell you is not pleasant, but you need to know...A few years back some Jazz lovers congregated at a Jazz bar just beyond the Marais, where a saxophonist was to play Stan Getz music, which I know you admire.

They didn't know each other. The event had been advertised in the papers and in various other locations around the city. Everyone had chosen to come and dine there, with friends and family, and listen to the music. It was going well, and everyone was chatting and tapping their feet animatedly, lost in the earthy, vibrant sound. They talked to each other as though they knew each other and enjoying their common love of Jazz.

Suddenly, there was the screech of an alarm and dark billows of smoke and flames appeared on the stairs. It all happened so quickly. People looked surprised, but soon their surprise turned to panic, as the fire began to engulf the diners and the wooden structure of the restaurant.

It was horrible – devastating. I remember the panic and screams as people realised it was reaching the bar and the restaurant – and fast. People began choking and gasping for air as the smoke enveloped them and overwhelmed their senses. Families clasped each other and tried to head for the door, tripping over the other eager diners as they did so, everyone was rushing to get out of the building. At this stage, no firefighters had arrived, no ambulances...

People cried out for help. I saw one old lady, lying next to her husband and crying. He lay totally still in the blackness. I fear he may have choked to death or had a heart attack. She wouldn't leave him, although many people tried to pull her away. She resisted, crying "If he dies, I want to go with him!"

I did my best, along with others to help the older folk escape. Many of the people there that night you now know as friends, Sienna. Lily and Alphonse, who I didn't know then, were celebrating their parents' anniversary. Their parents died in that fire. Alphonse had risked his life to save them but was lucky to escape with minor burns."

"Oh, I've noticed that burn on his arm..." Sienna said, sombrely.

"Theo was there with his partner, Daniel, who he'd known for a long time. He tried hard to save people, including Daniel, injuring his foot as he fell in the debris – hence his limp. Sadly, Daniel could not be saved. Theo also carried out Ernst's mother. His father died of smoke inhalation that night."

"But where was poor Ernst?" Sienna asked.

"He wasn't at the bar that night, Sienna."

"It's all so terrible!" Sienna exclaimed as a tear fell down her cheek and she stifled any sobs into her stiff white napkin.

"What about Freya and Mireille? Were they there?"

"Yes, they were, Sienna, but none of these people knew each other then. Freya was there with a boyfriend and they both got out, very shaken but mostly unharmed. He was badly burned, though. I saw him being carried to an ambulance as they ushered her in too. Mireille was there alone. She had come on her own but was also going to go upstairs later to see Belle, her dancer-friend who had a room over the bar. Sadly, she never got to see her, and Belle's remains were not identifiable. Mireille has suffered panic attacks ever since."

"Oh, I know, Xavier. This is so terrible. I've often wondered why everyone at the Jazz Club is so caring about each other..."

"We decided, quite a while after, of course, to create the club in honour of the Jazz lovers who died and as a support network for those who were left behind." Xavier replied, choking on his words. "We found someone who was willing to invest in it."

"What a lovely idea," said Sienna. "Was it your idea?"

"No – it was Ernst's," was the reply.

"But why wasn't Ernst at the bar that dreadful night?"

"Ah, well you see that's the problem. Ernst was due to go out, but he had a row with his father. He loved him dearly, but sometimes they clashed. We say things in anger that we don't mean. Ernst's parting words to him were 'and I don't care if I never see you again!' And he didn't get to."

"So, he's been living with that guilt ever since..."

"Yes, Sienna. It eats away at him like a cancer. It sends him into those dreadful black moods. Of course, it doesn't help his asthma either but that really is a separate issue – ironically that wasn't helped by smoke inhalation when he helped a friend put out a bonfire. I think he risked his life that night. Maybe he was trying to make up for what he felt he should have done at the bar? So, my sweet girl, now you know the whole story."

"But why couldn't he confide in me, Xavier?!" Sienna began to sob.

"He felt you might hate him and he told everyone you should not be told. He wanted to start again."

"Now he's gone! The fire wasn't his fault..."

"Ernst lost most of his self-esteem that night. He didn't believe he was good enough for anyone, let alone you. He's a sensitive soul."

The food arrived, but Sienna wasn't that hungry anymore. Xavier apologised profusely.

"*Oh-la-la*, what have I done? I should have at least let you enjoy the food but it all came pouring out. I'm so sorry, Sienna. Just pick at what you want, see it as just a small buffet. I didn't order much. Let me show you how to use the chopsticks, eh?"

Sienna fell silent. She ate some of the tasty food and remarked how delicious it was, but she was lost for words.

"Sienna?"

"What can I say, Xavier? I am shocked by what I have just heard. My poor Ernst. I used to tell him his fits of temper could land him in trouble."

"Well, I've broken the silence now. I will support you, Sienna. Maybe in a few weeks I could take you to the Jazz Club. Everyone knows Ernst has gone and they would love to see you again.

"Poor Madame LaFargue. She's lost them both." Sienna said, after a pause.

Chapter Twenty-Nine

Returning to her flat, Sienna got under her duvet and sobbed. She cried for what happened and she shed tears for what might have been. Then she got up, poured herself some of the expensive Chablis wine Xavier had given her and phoned Alphonse.

"Alphonse!" She sobbed, "I know what happened at the bar. Xavier has just told me..."
There was a pause before he replied. "Would you like to come over tomorrow? I have something for you, anyway. Now, try to get some sleep and know that we are all here to support you, *ma mignonne*."
Well, at least she would be seeing her trusty Alphonse. So, pulling the duvet tightly around her for comfort again, she said good night to the parrot, who didn't reply.
Sienna was up early. She didn't feel hungry but made some delicious coffee she'd bought from a little shop in Saint Germain the previous week, which sold coffee beans from all over the world, ground to perfection to your taste as you waited. She wasn't hungry but grabbed a small brioche and set off to see Alphonse. *At least all the walking you do in Paris is keeping my legs firm and trim*, she thought, *but no-one will be seeing them, sadly.*

"No," she said firmly to herself, "not down that route, Sienna!"
Her mother had once told her that self-talk was very useful, so she had taken to loudly proclaiming in her flat what she should and shouldn't do. *Good old mum! Should I tell her what's happened?* An inner voice said "no", because they would worry terribly. She had resisted telling her father anything so far, regarding Ernst.

Alphonse threw his arms around her in a reassuring, almost fatherly, manner.

"Come in and sit down, my dear friend. I know you've got to be so shocked, but we've all had to move on and sadly, *Chérie*, you must too. Ernst cannot forgive himself, but one day he will – who knows? It doesn't seem likely right now. He's a very sensitive soul and sensitive people read into and see things that are not there, sometimes. They feel things deeply. They hurt badly, and rejection scars them. Maybe he was just too scared of your reaction, although he actually did nothing wrong. It will be there, buzzing around his head, tormenting him."

"You sound as though you know, Alphonse..."

"My dear, I am a sensitive soul too, but my art is my outlet. It helps me express the deepest emotions. I lost both my parents that night. Come and see what I have for you now! Let's not dwell on the past today any further..." Alphonse produced a big package, exquisitely wrapped in delicate dusky pink paper, adorned with faded flowers, placed here and there on the thin, almost tissue-like paper. *So French!* Thought Sienna. She pulled open the broad, matching ribbon to reveal several wrapped items. The first turned out to be a box of watercolour paints.

"Wow!" She exclaimed excitedly.

"Yes, I've been to see Theo. These are not from his expensive artist ranges but are still good enough for you to use successfully."

"Oh, just look at the range of colours!" Sienna fingered them delicately. She pulled out a white palette, a putty rubber, a ruler and a box of pencils – all graded accordingly and well-sharpened. Lastly there was small collection of brushes.

"These, again, aren't sable, but are great for everyday use and you have most sizes you need there. The watercolour pad is there too – see!" Sienna was actually smiling again now.

"But Alphonse, it must have cost you so much! I will save and pay you back!"

"You will *not*!" Alphonse said, emphatically. "I'm doing well with my paintings and only last week sold one for a handsome sum. Can I not spoil my special friends, occasionally?"

"You are a dear, dear man, Alphonse..." Sienna was quite overcome and thrilled.

"Do you want to do some work today or just watch me?"

"I think today I will just watch you and learn. So, she lay on the sofa and observed as Alphonse put on his once-white, paint-stained tunic and looking every bit the Master Painter as he placed a large canvas on his easel. He looked at Sienna and moved his pencil around near her face, measuring and weighing distances between her delicate features.

"Oh no, Alphonse! Not today!" she laughed. "I have swollen eyes, unwashed hair and a nasty red spot that emerged overnight. Another day I may agree!"

He moved away and skilfully drew instead the outline of a landscape from a photo he had in one hand. Then he put the photo down and mixed the colours he needed on his well-used palette until he had exactly the right shade. He wet the paper all over and when it was still wet he dropped colour onto it, not just one, but several until they trickled down the page in a glorious melange of striking colour.

"Amazing!" said Sienna.

"This technique is called *wet-on-wet*. It's wonderful for loose, flowing paintings and abstract work. I often use it for skies which I paint, say, in blue or grey then I drop in the colour of the clouds – sometimes pink, sometimes yellow or purple in the sky. You can have a go next time you come if you'd like?"

"You are very talented, Alphonse – sickeningly so!" She laughed.

"You will be too, Sienna, but you must take it seriously and practice. Practice and more practice is the key as with many things! It's like playing the piano. You don't just sit down and play a Beethoven concerto, do you?"

Sienna left a couple of hours later, clasping her box of goodies. *Hmm*, she thought, *I think I'll buy a couple of tunics. At least I'll look the part...* She saw how immersed Alphonse was in his work and knew it would be the key to distracting her thoughts from Ernst and the whole horrible saga.

Chapter Thirty

It was soon daylight again. How quickly the days passed, and night turned into glorious day. The deep haunting depression had lifted. Sienna awoke feeling better than she had for a while. She seemed to have lost the empty feeling she'd had. Something had replaced it. It was the sense of being creative and a feeling of being able to make some plans again. Feeling out of control had been unimaginably awful but she now she wanted to paint. She could do it when and how she liked. It could be people or places that she painted – anything. It was wonderful to have so many choices, such freedom of expression. Of course, it would take a while and a lot of practice, but Alphonse had agreed that she could go twice a week. He enjoyed Sienna's company: she was talented and a keen learner.

After collecting baguettes from the boulangerie and meat from her favourite butcher Monsieur Martin, she wandered along to a dress shop where she'd seen a tunic and wondered if it was still there. The washed denim tunic hung in the corner of the boutique, as if waiting for her. Madame Boivin, the owner, fussed around her as she tried it on.

"I want clothes to paint in?" Sienna asked.

"*Mais oui, c'est pratique alors!*"

The woman produced two more tunics – another lighter denim and a natural linen-coloured tunic – and they all had large pockets in order to accommodate any erasers, brushes and the like: all her 'bits and bobs'. In fact, Sienna decided to take all of these and they would be her daily uniform with her trusty jeans. Madame Boivin smiled and gave her a small book as a gift entitled *Watercolour Washes*.

At home Sienna spent the rest of the morning experimenting with her new materials. She splashed on paint to make washes as Alphonse had taught her and, in her work, she found a new outlet of expression. Days and weeks passed, with Sienna still sad sometimes, but enjoying her ever-increasing number of students, who she taught in the evening from home. Her main passion was still her art and some days she could not wait to get started on her next project. Alphonse taught her twice weekly to draw; sometimes with pencil, sometimes charcoal and, lately, with pen and ink. Although she had an aptitude, her work needed refining. Alongside that she was becoming more and more confident with her paints. Sometimes, more so now the Spring-like weather arrived, she sat outside by the Seine and sketch the passers-by. She especially loved mirroring the people – young lovers, walking hand-in-hand, tired travellers sitting on benches or people dressed in unusual clothes or who maybe looked *different*. They all caught her eye. She would surreptitiously sit behind a *bouquiniste's* stand, not wanting to be noticed. However, one day, out of the blue, someone tapped her on the shoulder. She turned around and recognised the face. But no – it wasn't a friend, it was the old, crinkly and rather wizened face of an older man that she had just painted from a distance! He had been sitting nearby outside in the café opposite and she had been attracted to the character and 'lived-in' appearance of his face.

"My dear," he spoke in broken French, "I am on *en vacances* (on holiday) here from *Angleterre* and I see you have just – how do you say – paint me?" He tried to make himself understood in French.
Sienna laughed and replied, "I'm English too! Please don't struggle with your French!"
"I would like to buy the painting to take home, what do you say? I have a small gallery in Suffolk and I shall get it beautifully framed." He smiled…
Sienna was very taken aback, but he was sincere in his request and offered her a very generous sum. She wrapped it in some paper the *bouquiniste* gave her and he disappeared, still smiling.
"Oh wow! I've sold a painting, Alphonse!" She squealed down the phone, the minute she got home.
He laughed, "Sienna, darling, am I supposed to be surprised?"

Chapter Thirty-One

It was a typical Spring morning; at long last the many trees in the city were beginning to burst into life and the wintry light was being replaced by a more optimistic brightness. People would talk about 'Paris in the Spring' like a well-worn cliché, but Sienna felt the excitement of new beginnings all around her and in her soul. Looking through her window as she thrust it open, she breathed in the light, fresh air. By now, the cobbles were looking dry, and the puddle on her windowsill had all but disappeared. People walking by on their way to work wore smiles instead of heavy coats, although the air was still crisp, some had folded back the soft tops of their cabriolet cars and were playing music. Housewives were throwing bed linen out to air over chairs on their balconies or draping them over the windowsill. Washing lines were threaded across as bedlinen and shirts dried side by side in the soft wind. Sienna stretched and drank coffee. She donned her new casual clothes, deciding to only change if she was going to meet up with someone for lunch and the like. She looked down at her new brightly-striped socks – she felt good.

"Oh no! *Zut alors!*" One of them sported a large-ish, fraying hole already. She swore in anger.

"*Merde!*" squeaked the parrot in agreement. "Bloody things!"

"You've got to go, you stupid bilingual bird!" Sienna replied. Socks changed and wearing casual pumps, she was ready for the day. The phone rang – Xavier was calling.

"What are you doing today, Sienna? It's the weekend, thank goodness! Are you off to paint outside or to see Alphonse?"

"No, no," came the reply, "I'm not sure what I'm doing, apart from a few small errands."

"Look," said Xavier, "there's somewhere, strangely enough, that you haven't been to."

"Oh no!" she groaned. "Not La Tour Eiffel! I'm not a tourist, you know!"

"Shall I pick you up shortly after lunch?" She agreed happily.

Sienna suddenly felt a melancholic mood sweep over her as she put the phone down. *That should be Ernst*, she thought. The sunshine was now streaming through the open window and it made her think of the day at Fontainebleau. She remembered their laughter, their kisses and their strong declarations of undying love. That day always came back to haunt her. *Whatever has become of him?* The familiar deep ache which had been a constant companion came back in the pit of her stomach. She sat by the phone, as she had done before on so many occasions, willing it to ring and be Ernst. It never did. *I don't know where he is, I don't know who he's with and I don't know if he's well. Goodness, he could have died!* She did learn from Freya that his mother was sending him money so at least he wasn't a beggar and must be alive. *Maybe he had found someone else?* She tossed that thought away, saying loudly and defiantly, "No, Sienna! Not down that road!"

It was so sweet of Xavier to take her out. She knew he admired her greatly and if Ernst hadn't arrived on the scene, maybe their friendship would have developed further, but it hadn't. She shut the front door resolutely and went to buy meat, vegetables and fruit from her local shops, breathing in the fresh, energising air.

Later on, Xavier pulled up in his new white sports car – roof down, as Sienna had anticipated. He kissed her on the cheek and remarked how lovely she looked. The jeans and tunic had been replaced by smarter navy jeans over which she wore a long, roomy, thick sweater and had tossed a long scarf around her neck. She wore little make-up: just a dash of lipstick and mascara to show off her long, curly lashes. She was learning that less really is more in Paris!

"Drive on then, *James!*" She said, wondering if Xavier would wonder why she'd called him James. "It's such a surprise!"

It wasn't long before Sienna recognised the striking white dome of the Sacré Coeur ahead. She knew then and smiled.

"We're going to Montmartre! At last I shall see it!" When Xavier had finally found somewhere to park they negotiated the well-known steps that lead up to Montmartre, up to the well-trodden cobbled streets. Sienna was happy – tourist trap or not she had to see it. The renowned Sacré Coeur sat at the top, so they didn't get lost. Montmartre is a kind of village, Sienna knew, which had nurtured most of the great artists and sometimes writers of the past century. She and Ernst had discussed going there in the Spring.

"Right, let's go and sit down in the beautiful sunshine and 'people-watch' for a while?" Xavier suggested. "I'm afraid it's a bit touristy, but you'll cope!" Sienna skipped along towards a bench and quite naturally, without thinking, held Xavier's hand. Realising her mistake, as it was not Ernst of course, she blushed and withdrew it.

"Look Sienna! It really isn't a problem – if you want to hold my hand you can!"

She looked sheepish but by now they'd started walking again towards a little restaurant called Au Clairon des Chasseurs. It was nicely positioned in front of the Place du Tertre and overlooked the artists at work and the tourists of all nationalities jostling around. Some of them had already turned a reddish colour in the warm Spring sunshine. The owner brought their drinks outside and explained it was a very famous old restaurant, steeped in history. It was the haunt of artists, although it started as a place where *Gypsy Jazz* (in the style of Django Reinhardt) was played. This was particularly of interest to both of them, of course.

"See, Sienna! I knew you'd love it – artists and Jazz! What more could you want, eh?" She didn't reply, but he knew.

"Yes," the owner continued, "wandering musicians used to come and play here. You must come inside before you go and see all of the photos." This was all very exciting to Sienna's ears. Without thinking, she leant over and kissed Xavier on the cheek, and then blushed again when she'd realised what she'd done.

"I..." She faltered.

"I've made you happy, haven't I? Mission accomplished. Come now, let's go inside and then later we can move around out here amongst the artists outside."

It was good to get inside away from the many tourists, who were milling around with cameras and chattering away animatedly in various languages. They were greeted by rows of photos in one of the rooms. There were some in rather tired-looking but well-crafted frames, always depicting the smiling face of a musician from the past – many of whom were playing guitars. Sienna felt the sense of history in the room and the photos sparked a real curiosity about the musician's previous lives. In the photos, there were old, but comfortable-looking, leather sofas in deep brown hues which spoke of a past era. A group of photos on another wall behind them were possibly all famous writers or raconteurs, it seemed. One gentleman wore wire-rim glasses and was reading from a large, leather-bound tome. Another Sienna recognised to be a photo of Ernest Hemingway, wearing a favoured worn and weathered felt hat. This was brought to life for her as Sienna had just finished his book which was, of course, about his time in Paris. Further along were a few yellowed posters depicting the Moulin Rouge – and one of Toulouse Lautrec.

"All so interesting, Xavier," remarked Sienna, thanking him.

"Let's go and look at the artists outside, shall we?"

Tourists mingled with the painters. There were young students in distressed-looking jeans and rucksacks on their backs and tired travellers who sipped from flasks on the benches or low walls. A few of the youngsters sat in skimpy t-shirts enjoying some unseasonal sunbathing. Clearly some of the artists were just here to make a 'fast buck' and were churning out amusing, cartoon-like pictures of the tourists, hastily sketched in pen, pencil or charcoal. The true, talented and serious artists were sadly few and far between nowadays but usually had a small board beside them, stating their fee. People could pose for an hour or more sometimes as they produced skilled and accurate portraits for their delighted customers. Sienna looked enviously as they painted in the Spring sunshine.

Once they had their fill of exploring they made their way to Xavier's car, parked below, as the sun began to disappear behind the evening clouds, which had lost their usual grey, threatening appearance. They sat in the car for a while, drinking the juice they had just bought from a street-seller.

"I'm so glad, my lovely Sienna, to see you smile again." Xavier reached over and kissed her on her smiling mouth. Sienna recoiled, in surprise.

"Xavier, that was unexpected. I don't know what to say. I don't know if I'm ready to move on yet..."
Xavier apologised profusely. He had felt the moment was right, but it wouldn't happen again, he promised.

"I just want to see you happy, Sienna, that's all."

Chapter Thirty-Two

"Where are you? What are you up to?"
Freya's voice enquired on the phone, the next morning. "Are you coming to Jazz this week? There's a new mid-week session and you haven't been for so long, you'll see a few changes! We've all missed you so much, you know, but Lily and Alphonse have kept us informed.

I've been so busy at the shop, although, as you know, sadly it's not doing at all well. I'm just about to go out onto the pavement and place a few items outside for passers-by to look at; it usually attracts people in. I've got a couple of old iron benches they can sit on if it's sunny..." Updating Sienna eagerly, she continued, "You should get Xavier to bring you to the Jazz!"

"I'd like to come and meet up with you again, Freya. Long-time no-see!"

"Great. Hopefully see you there," came her reply.
Sienna arranged for Xavier to pick her up again, this time for the Jazz Club. She felt comfortable about their little liaison at Montmartre, as she knew Xavier wouldn't push anything.

"Sienna, you look stunning," he said as she got into the car. She had chosen to wear a short-sleeved, low-neck dress in a pale grey, with occasional floral interest here and there. She flung a deep pink wrap around her shoulders and felt 'quite French' indeed. As they arrived, they discovered the Jazz Club was jam-packed that night! The new mid-week session was proving popular, especially as the clement weather and lighter nights were on their way – it made the club easier to find, too. They made their way through the groups of people towards the bar. Lily came across to them; she looked stunning and very different in her mannequin-like outfit. Sienna gazed at her in admiration. She was wearing silver-coloured silk pyjamas with pointed black high-heels. Around her shoulders she had tossed a wide, tartan cashmere stole. She kissed Xavier and Sienna, clearly delighted to see them both.

"Where's Emile?" Xavier asked.

"Oh, he's here – over there chatting to the guy with the clarinet and the bushy beard!"

Lily and Emile seemed to make a delightful couple. Freya appeared next to them wearing so much jewellery that Sienna failed to see how she could walk. Gracefully, as ever, she danced to the clarinet music. The very skilful musicians relayed the music of Sidney Bechet and Albert Burbank. It was haunting and hypnotic slow Jazz, played effortlessly. Clearly masters of the clarinet, they made it look easy; their music echoed as a breathtaking sound which reverberated across the room, where lively dancers took to the floor in couples or stepped out alone again. Alphonse spotted Sienna and pulled her onto the small dance floor. It was a lively Jazz dance aptly called a Stomp – where you stomp your feet as you danced.

"You look fabulous!" said Alphonse. "Why don't you come over again during the week for another painting session?" After agreeing, Sienna wandered alone across the room to say *bonsoir* to Theo, who was chatting to Freya in the corner.

"So, Sienna, what do you think of the changes here?" Freya asked.

Sienna looked around. She spotted one of Alphonse's large portraits hanging in the corner. It was a stunning picture of a 1920s' lady. The inky hues were contrasted by the glimmering fabric of her bright pink dress. She wore a black velvet headband and carried a black cigarette holder. Her long beads gleamed as though real. Moving on further, Sienna noticed that some of the tables now had copper accessories, which shone against the rustic wood. The tasteful pieces had clearly all been co-ordinated by Freya. Part of the textured crumbling walls were now adorned with sun-faded flower prints and the small windows had chinks in their heavy curtains, where the blue-ish moonlight seeped through and hit patches of the room. The sensuous terracotta pots that housed huge, architectural and unusual greenery now had the occasional white flower poking through their dusky buds. *Only Freya could have put this together so cleverly and successfully*, Sienna acknowledged. *She was a woman of unusual, exceptional taste.*

Sienna smiled contentedly. This was her second home in Paris. Hélène was there, but there was no Henri. He'd sadly had to have a couple of months in rehab. Hélène looked relieved and was almost unrecognisable. She'd thrown off her former image and cut off the long plait that almost trailed to her waist. Her dark hair was cut short in a casual fashion, with a long, gappy fringe to her eyes. She wore large, round gold hoop earrings. With her dark complexion, she still maintained an exotic look.

"Poor Henri," remarked Sienna.

"His fault entirely," she replied. "I'm letting go of that one. What's happened to your Ernst? Another bad apple eh?"

Sienna lowered her eyes and, just in time, Xavier came over to pull her onto the dance-floor for the final slow dances of the evening. Holding her tight, he placed his cheek against hers as they moved around slowly to the romantic sound of the clarinet. She looked up at him and, for a moment, felt quite entranced by his laughing eyes and permanent grin. Somehow, it felt okay; she trusted Xavier. He brushed his finger gently across her cheek and she laughed, showing that deep and enticing dimple. Her eyes closed momentarily as she savoured the moment. The music finished to the sound of hand-clapping. Xavier fetched her wrap and, waving goodbye to everyone, walked arm-in-arm with him to the car. Sienna hadn't questioned it – it just seemed right. The car was parked at the end of the dimly-lit street just by the old lamp-post. They got in and Xavier asked, "May I?" before kissing her tenderly on the lips. This time she didn't pull back. She wanted him and kissing each other felt like the natural thing to do.

Arriving back outside her flat, Xavier thanked her for a wonderful evening.

"Xavier," she tentatively replied, squeezing his hand tightly. "It seems as though we've moved forward and yes... it is lovely... but I must do this at my pace or not at all. I do not feel ready to be intimate with anyone else yet..."

"That's fine, Sienna. I expected that. Can we not just enjoy each other's company and see what happens?" She nodded.

"*Tu es belle Sienna,*" he whispered as she got out of the car and ran up the steps. The moon shone its blue light on the steps and she could have sworn, as she looked up, that it was winking.

Chapter Thirty-Three

Alphonse was painting with acrylic today and spattering different colours, sometimes in Sienna's direction, as he smoothed the palette knife deftly over the canvas, creating layer-upon-layer of abstract splashes.

"Hey! Watch it!" Sienna laughed, moving her easel further along the window. She was just beginning a drawing of an old man she had sketched outside the week before. He was sitting on a bench outside, peeling an apple, his heavy-lidded eyes with deep bags beneath them, giving him the appearance of being half-asleep. It was probably the rays of the newly-arrived Spring sunshine that had bought him there that day. He had a book beside him, *The Great Gatsby* by Scott Fitzgerald – a writer friend of Hemingway – and the brightness of a keen intellect shone from his faded blue eyes, which in her sketch looked straight ahead, rather blankly. "May I sketch you?" Sienna had asked politely.

"*Mais, oui, bien sur.*" He gave a craggy smile, displaying just a few rather brown and crooked teeth at the top of his mouth, probably stained by numerous cups of coffee and lack of care. Sienna loved portraits, especially of 'characters' and unusual people. He took a swig from his hip flask. Sienna noticed his shirt looked as though it had once been of crisp, quality cotton, but its brown stripes were now fading, and its collar was creased and curled up at the corners. The old brown jacket he wore was reduced to one wooden button and hung shapelessly over a pair of green twill baggy trousers, which were turned up at the bottom haphazardly and hung over worn brown lace-up shoes.

"What's your name?" Sienna enquired.

"Ernest," was the reply. For a moment she misheard, and her skin had goose-bumps.

"Ernest!" he replied. "Like the writer. I was a writer too, you know!" he added.

"Really? Tell me more!" Sienna said, as she sketched.

"Well, you know the *Closerie des Lilas*, where the great writers used to meet. I took my notebook and spend many a day jotting down my thoughts. There were a lot of military people there in the early days. You know the sort who had seen war and proudly displayed their medals. They would tell stories and I jotted them down." He coughed uncontrollably and produced a large, crumpled handkerchief onto which he blew his nose noisily and then positioned it on his lap like a serviette. "And you, young lady? You're English, aren't you? Are you here to become an artist?"

"Well, I came as a language student, Ernest, but I've sort of ended up painting and giving a few English lessons in my spare time for cash."

"I can see you have a talent, my dear. Don't waste it. I ended up wasting mine. The whisky, you know. Work hard and you will sell your sketches and paintings. Get a little spot up in Montmartre when you have the confidence...although I've only spotted male artists there myself."

Delighted by the encouragement that day, Sienna was now engrossed in refining her sketch which she would then paint. Alphonse stopped work to answer the phone in the adjacent room. He returned looking sombre.

"What's the matter?" asked Sienna. "Has something happened?"

"I'm afraid it has. It's Mireille."

"Oh no, I didn't see her at the Jazz Club and was going to ring her."

"I'm afraid she's been caught shoplifting in Galeries Lafayette and it's not the first time, so it doesn't look good."

Sienna was surprised. Why would she do that?"

"Desperation leads us all to do irresponsible things sometimes. She has no money." Alphonse commented. "Work is sparse, and people are not keen to employ her because of the panic attacks which started after the fire, of course. Oh, that fire has a lot to answer for! To be fair, even before that she had money problems and did the same thing – without being caught. She told me the choice was either that or become a 'lady of the night' like her friend Belle, who danced with her at the *Folies Bergère*. She'll probably get a heavy fine like last time. She was with Ernst then. He paid the fine for her, then left her, unable to cope with the situation."

"Ah, so that's what happened. He paid the fine though." Sienna trailed off into thoughts of her own. "Always generous, Ernst was."

Alphonse sat down and poured himself a brandy. "I'm not sure what we can do, Sienna. It was Lily on the phone – she's going over to her flat to see her."

Sienna went home with a heavy heart. She had liked Mireille, despite her unflattering remarks about Ernst, and the fire had left a trail of misery for so many of the people she knew. Later that evening, she spoke to Lily on the phone, who had seen Mireille by then.

"She's in pieces, Sienna. She took some clothes from the shop but has returned them. However, the poor girl doesn't know where her next meal will come from. She is no longer in touch with any family, who seemed to have disowned her. They're in Nice, now, anyway. I have an idea though and I've put it to her. I don't know whether you know as I haven't seen you lately, but since my modelling days will gradually become less over the years as I get older, I'm starting a modelling agency. It is going to be very up-market and my Emile is investing in it, too," she explained. "Anyway, I will need a receptionist and I've offered Mireille the job. I think she will accept as we know each other well and she trusts me. It's going to be just off the Champs-Élysées near the high-end designer boutiques off the Avenue Montaigne. Mireille is bright and bubbly and good with people."

"Oh, Lily, you are an angel!" Sienna said. "You always have a big heart for those in trouble and you're such a loyal friend. Let me know how it goes. I must get in touch with Mireille.

Chapter Thirty-Four

Xavier had left a message on Sienna's answerphone that he needed to see her urgently. She didn't pick up the message but soon saw his white car pull up outside. She kissed him on the cheek and made him an *eau-de-vie* which was his favourite drink.

"You look exhausted, Sienna!"

"No, not really, I've been with Alphonse. Some days are just more challenging than others, and then she explained about Mireille.

"That's bad news," he said, shaking his head. "Maybe we could have a whip-round for her? Or would people not want to pay a fine. I guess she has to learn, poor darling. Keep me informed, won't you?"

"Luckily, Lily thinks she has a job for her."

"Sienna, I am the bearer of good or bad news – depending on the way you look at it. Spring has sprung and I'm off on my travels, I'm afraid. In fact, I have to pack tonight and drive straightaway down to Nice. There's urgent business to be done there and then afterwards I have to go and inspect some hotels along the *Côte D'Azur* elsewhere. I'm so sorry, but this is how my job works. I do love it, but I also love being with you. It will be a few weeks I'm afraid, and just as we were beginning to enjoy life together, eh?"

Sienna looked disappointed, but she knew about Xavier's job as it had been a bone of contention between him and Gabrielle.

"Look," Xavier said, putting an arm around her and pulling her close. "While I'm there I'm going to look at some yachts. As I told you, when my grandfather died I inherited quite a sum of money, a very substantial sum, in fact, and I've been thinking of getting a yacht in the South and an apartment or small villa. How would you fancy that? Holidaying by the Mediterranean and lying on my Sunseeker yacht, in your bikini?" He winked, and Sienna laughed. She couldn't deny it sounded good, but she was going to miss him. He kissed her tenderly on the lips and promised he would ring frequently. "I'm so sorry, *ma Chérie*, but I have to already go to pack."

Sienna felt numb: she couldn't quite decide how she felt about the situation between them.

The days and weeks went by slowly. Xavier was greatly missed but he seemed to be enjoying his travels. He had rung recently to say that as well as moving into a splendid apartment overlooking a blue, motionless bay near Antibes, he was also in the process of buying a navy blue and white Sunseeker yacht which was moored in the quiet nearby marina: a dream fulfilled. Sienna was walking through the Luxembourg Gardens, as she often did, and sat down on a bench and imagined what the summer might hold. She was, of course, supposed to be going back to England in August but she didn't want to think about that. The South of France sounded appealing and she imagined lying on a warm, sandy beach with Xavier or walking along in the evening holding hands and feeling the soft sand between her toes. She loved being with him. He would brighten her day and talk of positive, happy things. There were no brooding moods, just teasing and lively banter. It was too soon to know more. It held so much promise, but they were not lovers yet. Ernst had only been gone a few months, after all. Moving her thoughts deliberately to the tranquillity of her surroundings, she took a deep breath, inhaling the peace of this little haven, away from the bustle of the city. Time stood still here whilst she relaxed amongst the now-bursting flower beds and the aroma of blossoms. The horse chestnuts were in bloom along the tree-lined avenues. Everything looked rather elegant, rather than informal. The flowerbeds were interrupted by weathered statues, ponds and gravelly paths. The deep and often mottled greenery mingled with bright and unusual flowers such as the intense pink of the tulips which stood proudly upright in their beds, just like soldiers protecting the large main house behind them. On the opposite bed were early but tall and erect alliums, looking equally commanding.

For two days Sienna sat at home, just her and the wretched parrot (*why had she agreed to keep him?*). Perhaps he was company for her …in a very strange way! She felt tired and more than a little confused. She sat, a lot of the time in her flannelette English pyjamas, as they felt comforting. By day she drank copious glasses of water, and by evening copious glasses of wine. She didn't speak to anyone. She didn't answer the phone. The newspapers and post lay unread as she cosied up under a warm tartan rug belonging to her grandmother. *What should she do?* Ernst had gone, but did she really want to take it further with Xavier? Perhaps the idea that time would make her forget Ernst and fall in love with Xavier was not the truth? She felt Xavier would be extremely upset if she called the whole thing off. On the other hand, she knew she liked having Xavier around – he was lovely, cheerful, entertaining company, something she needed at the moment to fill the gaping hole that Ernst had left. She picked up the novel she was trying to read. The heroine had just broken up with her ill-fated lover, who then committed suicide. *Oh, yuck! Not what I need!* She tossed it aside, thinking the last thing she needed was more doom and gloom. Then it happened: the unexpected. The phone rang, and she decided that after two days she should pick it up. It was Xavier.

"*Chérie*, where have you been? I've been worried!"

"Oh, just a bad head cold Xavier, I could hardly talk."

"Listen," Xavier continued, "I have something to tell you. I've just been offered a permanent job here in Antibes by a different firm. Oh, Sienna, it's fabulous here and it's getting warmer by the day. I want to accept, but I want you here too. How would you like to come and live here with me? You'd love it..."

"But I'm due back in the UK at the end of August."

"Yep, I know, but you're French now and you belong here. We could go up to Paris and the UK for holidays. I will be earning a lot of money, so you won't have to work at all."

"You are amazing, but Paris is my home now. I am a Parisienne and this is where I belong."

There was silence at the other end of the phone, before Xavier asked, "Is that a definite no then? Look, Sienna, I know you're not in love with me, but sometimes it takes time. These instant attractions are often not real love."

From somewhere deep inside, Sienna plucked up the courage to say, "My dear Xavier. You are a wonderful man and one day you will make someone a wonderful husband, but that someone isn't me. I am in love with Paris."

"... and with Ernst, still," came the sad reply. "I've always known that, Sienna, but he's gone – goodness knows where. I know, though, that I would be second best and I respect your decision. I hope we can still be friends?"

"Of course, Xavier! Let's keep in touch from time to time."

"I wish you all the happiness in the world, my lovely Sienna, whoever that is with."

The phone line went dead. Sienna sat on the bed and sobbed. She hated herself for hurting Xavier, one of the best friends she'd ever had, and there was no guarantee she'd ever see Ernst again. She knew, however, that, despite everything, she couldn't have left Paris for good. Her heart was here now and that feeling wasn't going to go away easily.

Chapter Thirty-Five

Life had never seemed so empty. Sienna had some good friends in Paris, but two of them who'd been so dear to her had gone. She felt that she needed to get away from everything, but where to? Paris was where she belonged, and she definitely didn't want to go back to England. She spent her days painting, dreaming and planning possible futures. Sometimes she painted with Alphonse, sometimes alone. The nights seemed never-ending as she tossed and turned, checking the clock frequently, wondering what to do next and, often, wondering what Ernst was doing. Lily was a great support, as always, and she saw Freya often too. They got on really well and she admired Freya's courage in not lamenting the imminent loss of her space at the shop, as it was due to be sold soon. She just got on with life, travelling and selling her finds at street markets, *brocantes* and auctions.

  The intrepid Mireille seemed to have put her past behind her, after her heavy fine, and was doing very well as Lily's receptionist in her newly-appointed position in Lily's agency. It gave her a sense of importance and belonging. She'd even found herself a rather up-market boyfriend who spoilt her rotten and – by all accounts – adored her. She promised to bring him along to the Jazz Club one night and secretly longed to show him off. Sienna hadn't been to the little Jazz Club for a long time now; she found it impossible to imagine it without Ernst or indeed Xavier, but she missed its upbeat vibe and the effect on her mood. New people were coming all the time, but her heart just wasn't in it.

  The weeks passed as the Spring weather began to turn slowly into welcome Summer. Paris came alive, as people shed their wintry layers and smiled again. One night, sitting at home, putting the finishing touches to a sketch, she heard the phone ringing in the bedroom.

  "Sienna? Is that you? It's Theo," a voice said. She saw Theo occasionally, usually at the Marais either with

Lily or Mireille. He had a kind disposition and felt the pain of others deeply, which she admired.

"How lovely to hear from you, Theo!" Sienna said, with relief in her voice.

"I've a proposition for you," he said.

"Hmm..." replied Sienna. "The last time someone said that, they wanted me to go and live with them in the South of France!"

"Hah!" Theo replied. "But you know you're safe with me!"

"Safe as houses, Theo."

"My mother is here for a few weeks and she is going to look after my shop. I intend to go on holiday in Provence," he continued.

"Sounds lovely."

"That's just the point. Xavier has found me an idyllic place not too far from Aix-en-Provence which has plenty of rooms and I wondered if you'd like to come? Do you good, eh? I've also invited Freya and Mireille with her new boyfriend Michel. Lily can't come due to work commitments. How about it, then? It's too long a drive for me with my foot, so I thought we could take a train and hire a car there." Sienna mulled it over as he continued. "Look, think it over and let me know as soon as possible. I'll be off in about a week's time and the weather is getting warm there, so you'd better decide soon!"

Sienna felt honoured that Theo had thought of her and a holiday in the warmth sounded inviting. Provence, although she'd never been, sounded just the place to be if you were artistic as she would be able to paint and sketch, soak up the sun and socialise. She'd have her own space too, and time to explore the historical towns and villages. *Yippee!* The very next morning she returned Theo's call, saying she'd love to go and would start sorting out her belongings straightaway.

"Brilliant!" Theo replied. "I've asked the others – Mireille and Michel are going to give a lift to Freya. You can come on the train with me, if that's okay. We will all have a lovely time, though, and there are plenty of spacious rooms with excellent views and a pool at the back! I'll arrange for you and me to take the train to Avignon Saturday. We can pick up a hire car from there. Apparently, it's getting rather hot in Provence so pack the bikini!"

"Sounds amazing," Sienna said. "I won't be able to take my large easel though and I like to use it for my paintings."

"Don't worry, I've mentioned it to Mireille and Michel. They are happy to take it in their car. So, I'll speak again soon and sort the rail tickets out, okay? Bye for now."

The dusky hue of the morning sky became bright, clear and light as the train left Paris for Avignon. Sienna had a tingling feeling of expectancy as they passed through the French countryside towards the South. The feeling of escape from the hustle and bustle, the city smells, and the pace of Paris life was beginning to calm her already. The scenery of Burgundy and the Rhone Valley, with its vast vineyards that stretched as far as the eye could see, were a stark contrast of peacefulness to the sounds of police cars and fire-engines, the impatient horns of passing motorists, the screech of brakes and the loud shouts and chatter of the Parisians going about their daily lives. Everything had slowed down. It reminded Sienna of the slow pace in Norfolk where she'd been born but the scenery was much more interesting here. *Norfolk? Ah yes,* she remembered, *my parents would be coincidentally holidaying in Provence at the same time and it would be a great opportunity to meet up again.* She missed them. She started to tell Theo about it, but he had nodded off, so she put her head in a book, occasionally looking up to admire the verdant countryside or to drink some of the hot, strong coffee they had brought with them or to munch on a delicious baguette with saucisson.

Avignon was approaching as the train slowed down in the centre of a beautiful, quiet city, which was encircled by well-preserved stone ramparts. They gathered their luggage together and alighted from the train in the centre of town, the gentle heat hitting their faces as they walked from the station. Xavier had found them a spacious stone house up in one of the hilltop villages of Provence, which, by all accounts, had stunning views. Theo went to pick up the hire car whilst Sienna sat outside the station on her suitcase. She donned her large sunglasses and admired what she could see of the old city. The pace of life seemed leisurely and undemanding. She breathed in the clear, warm air. Theo appeared driving a small, grey Renault hatchback which he loaded up swiftly, grabbed a map and set off on what they hoped would be a new adventure. They drove in the direction of Aix-en-Provence, which Theo pointed out was well worth a visit.

Chapter Thirty-Six

Madame Bizieau, a plump but pleasant lady, greeted them warmly as they arrived eventually at the old, grey stone house up in the hills. She rented it out over the summer months and it had become very popular.
"*Bienvenue!*" she said. "Welcome to Provence," offering them some refreshment. "I believe some of your friends are coming tomorrow by car? Well, all of the beds are ready. There is a 'welcome' selection of food and drink in the fridge and I will give you directions to the nearest shops when you have settled in. Don't forget your bottles of water, will you? There is a maid who will come in to clean and change the beds, so you have nothing to worry about. You can relax." She raised a glass. "*Bonnes Vacances*, eh?! Just ring me if there is anything you need." With this, she disappeared into the distance, waddling purposefully, followed by a tiny, rather scruffy-looking dog. Theo changed immediately into a short-sleeved white t-shirt and light denim, slightly-fraying shorts. The shorts were to become his uniform for the next few weeks, replacing the habitual dungarees. He pinned his pony-tail back onto his head, grabbed his sunglasses and went outside to smoke a Gitane and unwind. Sienna put on a slightly creased, sleeveless linen dress with the obligatory flip-flops. She frowned at the sight of her white arms and legs which were only just emerging from their winter cover. She'd put a few things on hangers but, like Theo, she was eager to get outside and rest from the journey.

    She joined Theo at the back of the house in a well-appointed spacious courtyard, laid out with large stone slabs in differing shades of ochre, dusky pinks, soft warm greys and other off-white colours. The evening sun shone down on them, castling subtle shadows onto the courtyard and its deep green border of slender conical cypress trees. As she lay with legs out-stretched on a soft lounger, Sienna knew that this was going to be a very relaxing holiday and that they had chosen well. She looked around at her beautiful surroundings and smiled to herself. Already the smell of lavender mingled with rosemary wafted across the evening air, although it wasn't clear where it came from. It blended in with the pungent smell of other herbs and plants too for a delicious, intermingled aroma. The bright blue water of the pool beyond the courtyard was awash with the remainder of the day's sunlight. Beyond the pool were rows of dark green cypress trees, planted in clusters and forming a boundary to the hills behind them. Theo and Sienna lounged on ornate iron chairs which were placed around a round iron table in the courtyard. They were all arranged in such a way with the nearby plants and bushes to look like an extension of the living room; everything blended beautifully. Some plants were blooming brightly, and others had brilliant coloured heads, just poking tentatively out of their dusky buds. Others were in large terracotta pots and or in square, mottled silver zinc containers in differing shapes and sizes. To one side of the courtyard was a long rectangular dining table made of light grey stone with an amazing mosaic top in shades of ochre, grey and green, which dazzled when the sun came out. It was a large courtyard with benches and wooden chairs aplenty. These displayed masses of comfortable-looking cushions in bright, patterned colours. A few smaller empty pots were stacked here and there, holding the promise of more colour later in the season. Sienna hoisted up her dress as she stretched her legs up onto another chair and leant back on a large, plump striped cushion with her arms outstretched. There were roses climbing up the grey, plastered walls behind, which intertwined with bright red, happy-looking geraniums. An aged lantern hung to the side over a simple wooden garden bench which looked as though it had been there forever. It nestled beneath a large soft-green aromatic bush. Sienna and Theo agreed that this 'instant relaxation' was going to be extremely therapeutic. Theo lit another Gitane and stared up at the sky, drinking in the silence of the moment.

"Hello! Anyone at home?" Freya, Mireille and Michel had arrived, carrying enough luggage to last for several months, it appeared! They found Sienna and Theo splashing around in the pool. It had been a long and tiring journey for them, so they literally dumped everything on two of the beds and wandered around outside, stretching their stifled legs and taking in the surroundings.

"Come on in! The water's not cold!" called out Theo. They were all too tired to find their swimwear and change, so they grabbed some of the huge soft cushions and sat with their feet up, enjoying an ice-cold drink Sienna had produced from the fridge. They drank Pastis and Kir as they all chatted happily in the evening sunshine. Madame Bizieau had kindly made them a chicken casserole laced with garlic and rosemary, some salad and prepared various cheeses. Several bottles of *Côtes du Rhone* were on hand as well, as a surprise for their first evening together.

"*Que c'est parfait ici!* (It's perfect here!) Perfect!" squealed Mireille, squeezing Michel's arm until his face looked slightly flushed and a trifle embarrassed.

"Michel!" she said, imperiously. "Let's go and unpack whilst Sienna heats up the meal?"

Clearly not one to be told what to do, Michel lit another *Gitane* and poured himself more kir.

"Relax, Mireille! Let's just go and enjoy the remainder of the sun. There wasn't too much in Paris as we left." The subject had clearly ended. Sienna eventually served the meal on the long, stone table outside, as the sun began to disappear into an inky but glorious sky. The food was delicious and the 'vin rouge' lived up to its reputation as everyone laughed and giggled their way through what turned out to be more than enough for five people.

"Enough left-over wine for tomorrow?" Mireille suggested.

"Left-over wine Mireille?" Michel laughed…and poured another glass.

They staggered happily to their chosen rooms, with only the small catastrophe of Mireille wedging her stiletto between two of the large courtyard stones; luckily Freya saved the day by unwedging it.

Morning broke over the sleepy village and the sound of birds and stirring wildlife accompanied a hazy heat which gradually lifted to reveal the scorching sun in a cloudless sky. Everyone had gone out except Sienna, who had breakfast in the courtyard with them and then spent some time deciding what to paint as she took in the charming interior of the stone house. How fortunate they were to be here! She wandered around admiring the colours and furniture which together created the Provençal look with its easy charm. Muted colours were used with antique and rustic furniture, fashioned from natural materials such as stone, wood and metal. The unplastered walls could have looked cold and somewhat unwelcoming but were contrasted with the warmth of the terracotta in the room and it all assumed a softness. The floor was made of a warm-coloured wood too and there was an abundance of fine wood panelling around the room. There were exposed wooden beams everywhere and one section even had round cobbles on the floor, despite it being indoors. Sienna caught her breath. Only a very talented interior designer could have created this room. Cupboards, chairs, sideboards and side tables looked as though they had been made from reclaimed wood and had been softened with large pots of dramatic white flowers, speckled jars and large baskets. Two comfy putty-coloured sofas were adorned with bright, patterned throws and there were masses of check and striped cushions in varying shapes and sizes piled high on them.

Sienna was tempted to sketch the interior but decided to create a little group of items of her own outside. She put together a display of objects, haphazardly. She gathered pots, baskets and plants and arranged them together on the courtyard. The backdrop of the deep green cypresses added colour and style.

"Hey, what are you up to?" Theo appeared, now with a healthy-looking tan already which showed off the white of his even teeth as he grinned broadly. Running past Sienna, he dived into the pool, inadvertently splashing her nearby display.

"Go away!" Sienna cried, "or I'll get you to pose for me in swimming trunks!"

Theo grabbed a towel and raised his arms in mock surrender.

Chapter Thirty-Seven

Sienna pulled back the curtains sleepily, to reveal a sky that was a vast sheet of blue with not a cloud in sight. She yawned and, putting on a thin robe, made her way to the kitchen. The sound of Theo's rhythmic snoring echoed through the rooms. Though it was mid-morning, nobody had stirred yet but Sienna. There was only the sound of a small black and white cat as it jumped across the courtyard at the back and onto the windowsill. As she made some strong black coffee and arranged croissants, brioches and jam on the table, Theo and Freya appeared, both with bleary eyes and tousled hair.

"So, what are we going to do today?" Theo ventured. "I'd quite like to go off and explore on my own, if that's okay. Mireille and Michel are going to drive around a few of the villages."

Freya and Sienna decided to go to a neighbouring town as Freya needed some espadrilles and a few other items she forgot to pack.

"OK then, guys," Sienna said. "See you back here later on, but Theo please don't forget to buy some suncream. You look like lobster material to me." Sienna was just about to leave when the phone rang.

"Mum! Where are you? In Provence already?" Sienna answered.

Mr and Mrs Stevenson had driven across to Provence, which had been a two-day trip – but they clearly enjoyed it. They were staying in the beautiful historic city of Aix-en-Provence – which had once been the capital of Provence and were inviting Sienna and any of her friends to an excellent restaurant on the Cours Mirabeau, the fashionable main street.

"Lunch next Wednesday, then," Sienna agreed. "I'll see who else wants to come. It will be lovely to see you both again!"

"Oh, I'd love to come," said Freya with enthusiasm as she'd been listening in.

Freya and Sienna were ready to leave again. As they went to close the heavy wooden front door, the phone rang again.

"Ah, damn, this is just like Paris. I'd better get it."
"*Bonjour, Sienna. C'est Xavier*" her

"Xavier!" she said in surprise. Xavier explained that he had rung, hoping they could still be good friends and meet up whilst she was there.

"I'm not far away in Antibes and I could come over and see you all again. In fact, do you fancy a party? I've a bunch of interesting people who would love to come over and drink and dance with you all. What do you say to Saturday night? Ah, you have to ask the others? Of course. Just let me know and I will bring over my new friends and plenty of wine, of course!"

Sienna replaced the receiver and explained to Freya, who blushed slightly. Sienna remembered that Freya had always had somewhat of a crush on Xavier and was reminded of her sexy dancing at the Jazz Club when Xavier walked in. There was no doubt in her mind that Freya would agree to the party.

The girls intended to walk in the sunshine to a nearby market to begin with and then maybe get a bus to town. It was so refreshing to admire the colourful countryside as they passed by lavender fields and olive groves. The aroma of lavender filled the air yet again and the deep purple hue of the plants contrasted strikingly against the green foliage they passed. After a while, they sat on a bench and drank water, taking in the view. There was a road sign as they strolled through another quaint hillside village advertising a 'Wandering Minstrel' available to book.

"Look!" Sienna spied the sign. "Shall we ask him to come to the party?" They both decided it was a good idea and jotted down his number. It was around lunchtime, so it seemed like a good idea to go to a café to escape the sun at midday.

"You need more sun-cream on your shoulders," Freya warned Sienna. Freya had naturally tanned skin, but Sienna had to be careful.

"No, I'm fine," Sienna retorted, a decision she would later regret. After a light lunch in the shade and some time reading they went on to the market, quite glad to be rid of the flies that seemed to be circling around. Finding the market, which was along a main street, was easy – you just followed the noise and the smell of food cooking.

The stalls sold everything in a rather haphazard manner, from silver jewellery, barrels of shiny olives, t-shirts and rustic loaves to sausages and other warm delicacies, sizzling away in large, heavy pans. Freya espied a stall that had multi-coloured sandals and espadrilles and the result was they both walked away having acquired bright new shoes each. Sienna snapped up two skimpy bikinis in startling colours before they decided to wander back to the house. Once they arrived, having walked back along the dusty tracks, Sienna espied herself in a long mirror and reeled at the lobster red skin around her chest, across her shoulders and tops of her arms, which she hastily covered in after-sun lotion.

"Uh-oh!" she declared.

"Told you so." Freya laughed. *It looks like tomorrow is going to be a quiet day sketching – but in the shade!*

Theo returned from an excellent days sightseeing. He had driven through lavender fields along to the pine forests which had been bathed in sunlight and looked a spectacular sight. He told Sienna that it was indeed an artist's paradise; it was, of course, the colourful scenery that had charmed the likes of Cezanne and Van Gogh. Sienna felt spurred on to get her easel out and ready for the next day.

Freya and Sienna had returned from their walk, happy with their new possessions and glowing with the fresh tan on their faces and bodies. The air felt good here; Paris could be very stifling when it was hot. Sienna rang the 'Wandering Minstrel' and booked him straightaway.

Tomorrow they would plan and fetch some things for the party. Sienna explained to Freya that Xavier would be bringing lots of booze and things to eat, as well as several of his new friends, who, by Xavier's word, would be good fun to be with.

"Ah, but what about music?" Freya asked.

"Good point," Sienna replied. "I will sort that out tomorrow too. Perhaps you'd like to help?"

The week passed by quickly. They splashed and swam in the pool and walked around admiring the sloping vineyard along the hills, stopping off at little cafés along the way. These cafés were often very basic but steeped in tradition and served tasty home-made Provençal dishes. Saturday couldn't arrive quickly enough: it promised to be a lot of fun.

Chapter Thirty-Eight

A familiar, shiny-white cabriolet pulled up outside with the roof down and several people in bright t-shirts, hats and sunglasses alighted, all clutching baskets of food, bottles of wine and other delicacies. They looked to be sun-tanned and in high spirits. Xavier brought Jean-Luc, Claude, Serge and Marie-France and loaded the boot with goodies for the buffet-style soirée. Xavier embraced Sienna as she opened the door. "It's so good to see you again, Sienna!"

"Likewise, Xavier." She smiled. "I've missed your banter – and you, of course."

Going backwards and forwards to the car, they unloaded the wine and food first before proceeding to unload sleeping bags, beach towels and changes of clothes from the roomy boot. After a quick wash, they all sat outside and enjoyed the remains of the late glow of the afternoon sun with a glass of Pastis and plenty of water to quench the dehydration of the journey. Xavier introduced Jean-Luc, who was a striking young man with black hair, a deep tan and an engaging smile. They found out in conversation that he was, in fact, a successful interior designer who had worked on Xavier's new abode in Antibes.

Claude was a slightly-built and almost 'beautiful' with his long, curling eyelashes and single silver earring. His brown hair was cut in a very avant-garde style and had little flashes of lighter colours flushed through it. He, unsurprisingly, turned out to be a hairdresser. The girls were delighted to meet him and immediately moaned about what the chlorine in the pool and salt in the seawater had done to their shiny locks. Serge proved to be an estate agent, with his own business. He was very much a people person and addressed them all constantly by name in a way that made them feel he was interested in their lives.

"Tell me, Freya," he had asked, "how do you manage to race around the country buying heavy items of furniture? Do you have a van or what? It must be quite exhausting sometimes..."

Last but not least, Xavier introduced the beautiful Marie-France who looked as though she lived in a gym (turns out not so, she just walked an awful lot as per the custom of French women to keep trim).

"Marie-France, what do you do for a living? Are you in Antibes?" Serge asked, clearly not yet properly acquainted, although they just spent an hour or so squashed together like sardines on the back seat of Xavier's car.

"Me? Oh, I'm a writer," she smiled. "I work for a magazine in Paris and I'm just down here for a month on holiday."

Sienna introduced Theo, Freya, Mireille and Michel and the conversation flowed until it was time to sort out the sleeping arrangements and change for the evening. Xavier and Sienna sorted out the buffet. He'd had the wisdom to bring plenty of throw-away plates to save on washing up. The white wines and some drinks that needed chilling were assigned to the fridge and the long table outside was covered in a large blue checked oil-cloth 'á la Provençal'. The amount of food was almost overwhelming with both Xavier and Sienna anxious to deliver a pleasing spread. The choice seemed to be never-ending. At the end of one of the table were savoury dishes such as 'tapenade' – an olive dip made of black olives, capers, anchovies, garlic and olive oil served with croutons. Besides that, was a delicious-looking quiche and a plate of *Fromage de Chèvre* (goats cheese) to eat with the quiches and tarts. Tasty salads sat alongside warmer meals such as *bouillabaisse*: a minimum of four different types of fish cooked in stock with onions, tomato, garlic, saffron and herbs. There was a large dish of 'daube' looking equally tempting – this was a Provençal stew with vegetables and braised in red wine. As a light meal, you could eat *Omelette aux Truffles*. Everything had been transported carefully from Xavier's local restaurant and Sienna's favourite places to buy home-made Provençal food. For dessert, there was a choice of *Clafoutis de Cerises*, a delicious cherry dessert, the famous *Moeulleux au Chocolat*, the obligatory chocolate dessert or *Tiramisu aux Apricots*, an apricot tiramisu. Xavier smiled broadly as he brought out a *Tarte Tropézienne*, the signature cake of Saint Tropez, a dish filled with orange flower-flavoured cream and quite delicious. He had spared no expense as the guests enjoyed some of the famous *Pouilly-Fuissé white wine* and *un bon Côtes du Rhone*.

Sienna, with a glass in hand and eyes sparkling, pronounced a toast to the guests and introduced some early evening entertainment in the form of the "Wandering Minstrel" she had booked. He arrived dressed in an old-fashioned folk costume, bearing various musical instruments and accompanied by a young child who put an old tin beside them, which was presumably for donations. The Minstrel, resplendent in ochre and burgundy, proceeded to play a small flute and dance with the child to a merry tune which caused everyone to clap in time with the music. He also had a violin and a small guitar, which he played enthusiastically and interspersed the music to recite poems and tell a story. The story, spoken in rapid French and in a certain Patois (accent), made everyone laugh– except Sienna, who hadn't understood a word but didn't care at all as she raised a glass. It turned out to be that he hailed from the old troubadour country of Toulouse, well-known for its wandering and talented minstrels through the ages. It was a refreshing interlude, and everyone threw coins and notes into the child's tin, which she picked up and clutched close to her chest, like a treasured toy, and left smiling with the father, who had bowed, raised his felt hat and made his exit.

The music and the noise of the revelry became quite loud as the evening progressed but as there were no direct neighbours, it didn't seem to matter. The wine flowed and the mood mellowed. Sienna sat on cushions on the floor, deep in conversation with Jean-Luc about his job, her art and Paris mostly. Theo disappeared off at some stage, along with Claude, and were not seen until the following morning. Mireille and Michel danced closely and slowly to the slower tunes. Marie-France and Serge took great delight in donning swimwear and messing around in the pool, which looked blue and inviting long into the evening. Sienna thought she would have a wander outside with Jean-Luc as it began to get dark. Marie-France, glorious in a tiny red bikini was jumping up and down in the water with Serge, wine glass in hand. As Sienna walked across the courtyard she heard a rustle behind a group of conifers in one corner. Walking past with Jean-Luc, she turned to glance at the trees and saw Freya with Xavier, kissing and caressing each other rather fervently. She was startled, but as the reality sank in, she was relieved that she didn't actually feel any jealousy. She just felt happy that Freya had finally got her man, so to speak. She sat down again on the cushions with Jean-Luc and then it happened. Jean-Luc pulled her close and kissed her. The wine worked its magic and she responded teasingly by pulling away and then bending forward and kissing him again, more passionately.

When the evening came to a close with various couples retreating to their rooms or cosying up in the living room in sleeping bags or nestling between the largest plumped up floor cushions. Sienna led Jean-Luc to her bedroom, the room spinning somewhat as she bumped into furniture along the way. Jean-Luc seemed equally inebriated and stumbled along with a silly grin on his face.

"Please close that curtain again!" Sienna begged as the morning light streamed into the bedroom through an opening in the curtain. Her head was pounding as she rolled over and saw Jean-Luc snoring heavily beside her. *Oh no! What have I done? This wasn't meant to happen at all!* Sienna staggered to the kitchen and made two very strong black coffees for herself and Jean-Luc. She sat down on the bed, clutching her cup of coffee closely as though it was life-support, as Jean-Luc stirred.

"Jean-Luc," she asked nervously. "Please tell me... I have to know... er, did we... er?"
He had not been quite as tipsy as Sienna. He laughed.

"Sienna, I am a gentleman and you, my dear, are still fully clothed. Have you not noticed?" She felt her body beneath her dress and checked nothing had been removed, heaving a sigh of relief. Her head hurt as she asked him what did actually happen.

"I tucked you up into bed and you fell asleep at once – a bit too much *Pouilly-Fuissé*, I think!"

She knew it had to be the truth and was relieved. She liked Jean-Luc immensely and found him devastatingly attractive, but she knew that she couldn't cope with one-night stands and had been true to herself, if not a trifle riskily. They laughed as they drank a lot of water and gradually decided to open the heavy curtains and welcome the dazzling Provençal daylight. The sound of an engine starting up startled Sienna as she looked out. Xavier and Freya were off for a spin in his car, it seemed. *Dear Xavier,* she thought, *he deserves some fun and Freya is very vibrant and funny.* They headed out of the bedroom towards the kitchen to wash up their cups.

Theo emerged with a bleary-eyed Claude draped around him and both clutched large fluffy towels. They chased each other to the pool and spent the morning frolicking in the water like children. Mireille and Michel had awoken early and gone for a long walk. They hadn't drunk so much the night before, like the others. Marie-France appeared to have spent the night with Serge, although no-one was quite sure, as they didn't appear to be an item the next day.

"Looks like a good time was had by all!" laughed Sienna to Jean-Luc as they began cleaning away and washing dishes. Xavier appeared a couple of hours later with a beaming Freya on his arm.

"Guess what?" he said. "Freya has agreed to come home to Antibes with me and spend a few weeks travelling and on my boat on the Med." He then proudly produced a photo of the navy blue and white yacht (he didn't mention the unknown young lady in a skimpy bikini stretched out and sunbathing on the deck).

"But we're leaving for Paris after I've seen my parents during the week and Freya has a lift back with 'the two M's,"

"No problem. I'm coming back home soon and will bring Freya home."

"Home?" Sienna asked. "Your home is here now, Xavier!"

"No," he replied. "I'm a Parisian through and through – I get homesick for Paris. I've decided to keep the flat and boat for holidays, although I will probably rent the flat out in between. I'm going to get another apartment in Paris." Sienna said she was delighted that he would be coming back to the Jazz Club. Freya just smiled...

The holiday was coming to a close, but Sienna wanted to meet up with her parents in Aix-en-Provence first. Theo said he'd like to come and would drive them there. Claude had returned to the Riviera with Xavier but was planning to spend some time with Theo in Paris in the near future. They seemed to be getting on well and Sienna hadn't seen Theo look so carefree for a long time. The extra bounce in his step, the enthusiastic manner and the way he laughed betrayed a man who might well have been in the first throes of *l'amour*! They set off for Aix in the little Renault, having agreed to meet Mr and Mrs Stevenson on the main street, the 'Cours Mirabeau'.

Aix was stunning and embraced a slow pace of life which reined you into its calmness. There were plenty of folk around though; it was a thriving town. The 'Cours Mirabeau' proved to be the *place to be seen* – where fashionable people posed on pavement terraces and drank coffee. It was a leafy boulevard which boasted public squares and several well-appointed fountains. Mr and Mrs Stevenson were sitting outside the bistro at which they had agreed to meet, looking tanned and relaxed. They got up immediately and hugged Sienna and shook Theo's hand in a true English way. The Stevenson's were relieved and happy to see Sienna appearing happy and even slightly tanned, despite her pale skin. Her phone calls around the time that Ernst had disappeared had concerned them greatly, but she seemed fine now. They chatted animatedly over a light, but delicious Provençal lunch in the little bistro *La Cigale* and were interested to hear about Theo's art shop. Mrs Stevenson painted herself, but only with a local Art class and she was tremendously proud of Sienna's gift.

"So, when are you coming back in August? So we can arrange our diary," she enquired. There was an awkward silence.

"Mum, I don't know if I will be coming back. If I can sell more paintings and teach more students, I may stay. I love Paris and would miss it so much if I were to leave. But who knows? A lot can happen between now and then." As it always had in Sienna's life.

Chapter Thirty-Nine

The journey back to Paris was uneventful, with Theo nodding off (with a small smile on his face) for most of it. Sienna sat reading a book about Hemingway's time in Cuba. Part of her didn't want to go back to her life without Ernst. It was easier to bear now though. The old cliché about time being a healer was partly true. The rawness had gone but the memories played havoc with her night-time thoughts and dreams now and then. Back at the flat, she left Theo to make his way home in the taxi, thanking him for a memorable holiday. She had enjoyed every minute and the laughter and companionship had done her good both physically and mentally. She popped around the corner to collect the parrot, who had amused the family who looked after him greatly and learnt some new words too. The flat seemed quiet and lacking in atmosphere, so the first thing she did was to turn on the radio and make it feel like home again. Her bed looked welcoming, though, as she remembered that there's nothing like one's own bed when you've been on holiday. She left her case in the bedroom to be unpacked later and curled up on the sofa with a drink. After an hour or so, Sienna decided to ring a few friends and find out the latest news. Lily would be her first port of call, of course. As she went to the phone, it rang, uncannily.

"Sienna, it's Lily! Have you had a wonderful time? We must meet up, I want to hear all about it. Firstly, Sienna, I'm afraid I have some sad news. Sit down please."

"What is it? Is it Alphonse? Are you OK?"

"Yes, we are OK. Remember the neighbour who was Madame LaFargue's friend and took her to get herbs?"

"Yes – you mean Ernst's mum's friend?"

"Well, yesterday she went in to take her some fruit from the market and saw her sitting outside, soaking up the glorious sunshine in her lovely garden. She didn't want to wake her, as she'd dozed off, but she soon realised.

Sienna, Madame LaFargue has died. She died alone in her garden, surrounded by her birds, herbs and the flowers she so loved."

"Oh no, no!" cried Sienna. "How awful: she wasn't old. Does Ernst know? Poor Ernst."

"Yes, he knows, Sienna. Jeanne, the neighbour, was the only person apart from his mother to have a contact number. She had been sworn to silence but Madame LaFargue had left instructions in case anything happened."

"*Quelle horreur, Lily!* What happened to her? I remember that when we were last there she looked rather pale and vulnerable, but she wasn't ill I don't think..."

"No," Lily replied. "The doctor thinks it was all very peaceful. She simply sat down in her garden and had a heart attack. I don't know any more. Are you okay? I know she was very fond of you, Sienna."

"Oh, she was a lovely lady, but I didn't like to contact her as Ernst wanted a clean break."

"She's left a letter for Ernst in case anything happened."

"He will be devastated..." Sienna said slowly.

"I know," Lily replied. "I will ring you when I know more. I had stayed in touch with her from time to time since the fire. Now, sleep tight, *Chérie*."

Sienna put the phone down slowly and regretfully. She wished she'd gone to see her. *Would Ernst come back for her funeral?* Thoughts raced through her mind. She poured out a whisky (which she saved for emergencies) and then another after. *How could such a wonderful holiday end so abruptly and sadly?*

Sienna awoke feeling sad and more than a little confused. Should she go to the funeral? She was very fond of Madame LaFargue but...*would Ernst be there? Was it the correct thing to do?* She rang Xavier to tell him the news. He was extremely upset; he had known Ernst a long time and had found his mother a delightful and interesting lady.

"That's so sad, Sienna," he said, forlornly. "Would you like me to come back for the funeral? I could postpone my holiday and Freya will understand. Ernst was a good and trusted friend. He just lost his way, somehow."
Sienna felt confused again. *What if Ernst turned up and she was there with Xavier?* She thought it might confirm Ernst's previous suspicions of a liaison with Xavier and not only ruin their memories but show her to be a liar. She wasn't sure what Ernst's, sometimes twisted thinking could do to him at a time when he was mourning his beloved mother. She decided to explain it all to Xavier when she rang him back later. Xavier was a straightforward kind of man and could see it might cause a problem for his old friend.

"He was just always so suspicious of us, Xavier."

"Okay, *Chérie*," he replied. "You go to the funeral with Lily. She will want to go. We will stay in touch, eh? I've just told Freya, she's really sad and sends her love."
Sienna was not too comfortable with going to the funeral at all, but she thought Ernst would have to be very brave just to suddenly turn up so maybe he wouldn't be there at all. Somewhere, deep down inside her, she hoped that he would. At the least they could perhaps clear the air; she had felt deeply hurt at what he did. There was anger that still lingered at his not being able to confide in her about the dreadful emotions he suffered. There was even more anger at his leaving without warning. This latest happening would surely leave him in an even worse mess – but still she had hope.

"What a horrible thing to happen!" she said out loud.

"*Merde!*" echoed the dratted parrot behind her, who had no idea of what was going on.

The next day rained and Sienna's mood was echoed in the weather. Lily rang with further details of the funeral, which was to be held in a few days' time. It seemed to be very quickly arranged but Sienna found out that was the way they did it in France. Madame LaFargue's brother, Jean-Pierre, was organising everything with his wife. The flowers would only be from family. Sienna had a chic black suit she had bought in Paris as it looked useful, which she was to team with her grey silk blouse and the silver choker that Ernst had bought her. The day arrived quickly and Lily picked her up in her small Fiat, to drive over to the small Catholic church, just outside Milly-La-Forêt. Sienna felt apprehensive, but it had to be done. She had bought a simple card of condolence to give to Jean-Pierre but didn't want to attend the gathering afterwards which was for drinks and nibbles in a local bar.

The church was crowded. The coffin was brought in, scattered with beautiful Spring flowers, interspersed with tiny green herbal arrangements. Apparently, there were several old friends of her husband and some of his former drinking buddies there with their wives. A few of the people from the awful fire were there. Sienna saw Theo, Alphonse and Mireille but may have missed others. There were people that Ernst's father had worked with, old school friends, ladies who lived in the nearby villages, painters and decorators and an odd-job man that Madame LaFargue employed. Everyone was smartly dressed and in dark colours, mainly black. Sienna, feeling a touch shaky, scanned the rows ahead of them, as they sat at the back. She couldn't see anyone that resembled Ernst. She repeated this several times but as the church was small she concluded he wasn't there. Lily knew her angst and held her hand for a while. *Why hadn't he come? His own mother whom he loved so much?* The service was short and Lily and Sienna escaped the throng outside by going to a local brasserie. Sienna looked at her watch an hour later and sighed with relief, knowing it would all be over now.

"Did I do the right thing in not getting in touch with Madame LaFargue?" she asked Lily, who replied, "It was a difficult situation."

"Lily, I think I would like to buy a few flowers and place them on the grave before we go."

Later in the day, armed with flowers, and with Lily sitting patiently in the car, Sienna went back to the grave. She saw a bent figure in a dark overcoat, kneeling at the grave. It stopped her in her tracks. Sienna was a great reader of romantic and mystery fiction and she suddenly remembered a scenario where the loved one wasn't at the church but turned up at the grave later. *Was that why she had the idea to go there?* She didn't know. She approached the grave gingerly with a lump in her throat. He heard her approach and turned around – but it wasn't Ernst. She didn't know what she felt; relief, sadness and all kinds of emotions enveloped her as she said *bonjour* to the stranger. She learned that he had been an old school-friend of Ernst's who had spent many happy times at the LaFargue's former home.

"My train was delayed and sadly I missed the funeral. I haven't seen Ernst for years, but I saw that his mother had died and thought it might be nice to come and see him. Where is Ernst, though?"

"I really don't know I'm afraid. I think he is working abroad now..." Not wishing to prolong the conversation, she placed the flowers on the grave and hurried back to the car with tears in her eyes.

Xavier, ever thoughtful, sent her flowers that she found as she arrived home. It made her feel safe that he was always there for her, even at a temporary distance. *Dear Xavier*, she thought, *he's so supportive.* She knew a call to him later would lift her mood – and it did. She began thinking of Provence again, of summer clothes, bikinis and flip-flops, of the laughter and the party. Nothing had changed in her life really. She picked up her sketch pad and charcoal and drew the parrot, who mercifully remained still and quiet.

Chapter Forty

A couple of days later Sienna put on her 'work gear' and got ready to go over to Alphonse's. She grabbed her paints and everything she needed for another day working hard but just as she was about to leave, she heard the phone. *That phone again!* She thought, realising it was, in fact, a blessing that people rang her so often.

"Oh, hi Sienna! Lily here again! Are you doing anything today?"

"Well, I was just going to finish off a painting at Alphonse's place."

"Could it wait? I really need to talk to you. Could you meet me at Le Petit Lapin in Saint Germain in about an hour?"

"I guess so, Lily. I can paint later – see you then."
Sienna thought that Lily might be in trouble with her boyfriend, as it had been a somewhat rocky road lately. She owed it to Lily to help her in a crisis as she'd been so good to her. Changing out of her slightly paint-splattered tunic, she put on a new Spring dress she had espied in the little boutique around the corner. It had three-quarter sleeves, a rounded neck and a full skirt. Her tiny waist was emphasised by a wrap-around tied belt. The pink of the dress showed off her light tan and she felt good in it. Arriving at the brasserie, she could only see a couple of people outside, so she went in – there was just a man engrossed in a newspaper. Lily was unusually late, so she ordered a café crème and sat down inside, reading a chapter of a novel she just started.

"May I join you?" A familiar voice resounded to the right of her. She looked up to see Ernst, looking tanned and smiling.

"*Mon Dieu, Ernst!*" she cried out in surprise. "Is it really you? You're meant to be Lily. *Qu'est-ce qui se passe alors?*" ("What's going on?")
He paused. Looking serious, he replied, "Look, if you don't want to talk to me I quite understand and I will go?"

Sienna caught her breath and mumbled something he didn't catch. Her knees trembled.

"Forgive me, but I asked Lily to lure you here as I didn't think you'd come otherwise and you'd have every right not to, Sienna. I haven't treated you well. Will you hear me out?" he continued, seriously.

"You weren't at your mother's funeral, though? I'm so sorry she died..."

"Yes, I came to be there, but at the last moment I couldn't face everyone and Lily said you'd be there. It was good of you. I've just been to the churchyard to say goodbye. I'm broken-hearted, Sienna. I would have come, of course, if I'd known she was ill." A tear fell down onto his tanned cheek.

"Can we talk, please, Sienna, or do you hate me?"

"Hate you?!" Sienna replied. "How could I ever *hate* you? What you did hurt me badly though and I'm still scarred by it."

"I have so many regrets. There is a story, though, that I should have told you about."

"If you mean about the fire, then I know! Xavier has told me everything. It's dreadful what happened and losing your father so tragically too..."

"Yes, but I wasn't there to try to get him out."

"I know, Ernst, but it wasn't *your* fault that he died! You cannot blame yourself for having that row with him and saying you wished him dead. It wasn't a very nice or clever thing to say, but Ernst, the fire was not your fault."

"I know that now, but then I didn't. I was so dreadfully insecure. I've had months to sort my head out. I've been living in Corsica and I found work there at the Club Med by the sea. The temperature is always warm or hot there and my asthma has practically gone. It took a while to relax, but I began swimming, diving and snorkelling every day and resting on the beach. When I had enough money, I went to a psychologist who helped me with my problems and my unfounded guilt. There's still a bit of work to do with my anger, but otherwise I feel like a new man. I like myself for the first time ever. I'm healthy. Healthy? Well, I lost you – and now *Maman*..." his words trailed away.

Sienna didn't know what to say.

"I don't suppose there's any chance of forgiveness, Sienna?" Ernst asked. "I know what I did. I regret it so badly, but I really was a mess. I didn't know who I was, what I wanted to do. The only thing I knew was that I loved you, but I would never be good enough. I left you with love and it almost killed me. I even thought of suicide. I just wanted you to be free to have the happy life you deserve."

Sienna looked down and felt tears welling up in her eyes.

"Look, Sienna, I have to go now. There's so much to be done over at *Maman's* house. I shall be there for a while. You know where I am if you want me; I will leave it to you. I will understand if you don't come. By the way, you look sensational." He planted a kiss on her cheek, tentatively.

"Are you going back to Corsica?"

"I don't know, Sienna. I haven't handed in my resignation, though." With that he left.

Sienna was in shock; she didn't know what to do. She sat breathing in the waft of his familiar aftershave that he always wore. She felt stunned and a tad shaky. *Whatever am I do to do?* she asked herself. Her heart was telling her the thing she didn't want to admit to: she still loved him.

The next day Sienna met up with Lily at her flat.

"I do hope you're not angry at me for what I did?" Lily asked anxiously.

"My dear Lily," Sienna replied. "How could anyone be angry with you? You knew, didn't you? You knew I never managed to get over Ernst! How can I be angry with him? He was so mixed up and torn apart by what he'd said to his father."

"How is he now?" Lily asked.

"He looks fantastic, so well and tanned. He seems to have sorted himself out. What am I to do?"

"Sienna, you know what you have to do. Take my car for a few days. Go and see him. See what happens..."
It was the push Sienna needed – she hugged Lily tightly. She set off for Milly the very next morning, hoping she'd find him in.

Chapter Forty-One

The little Fiat pulled up in front of Madame LaFargue's quaint cottage. There was no car outside – but then Ernst may have sold his car. Sienna was about to grab hold of her overnight bag and then knock on the door, but then realised it might look somewhat presumptuous so she left it in the boot and walked towards the door, inhaling deeply. There was no reply to her knocks. For a moment she wondered if he might have gone back to Corsica; she hadn't exactly fallen at his feet, after all. She went to the side-gate and looked over into the tangled garden. She knew if she looked deeper it wasn't really tangled and overgrown – it had been purposefully arranged as a 'cottage garden', tousled and informal. She loved this garden and the cottage. Just then, she heard the crunch of footsteps on the path behind her and someone put their hands over her eyes.

"Ernst!" she turned around and he was grinning broadly.

"I knew you'd come," was all he said, as he placed a kiss lovingly on her cheek and put his arm around her, ushering her into the cottage.

"I thought you'd gone, Ernst..."

"Well, I must admit I felt pretty deflated when I heard about Xavier. Are you still together?"

"How do you know about that...? It's over, Ernst; it was a while back now. It was never going to last – it's always been you. I didn't want anybody else."

"I know that it was Xavier," he replied wistfully. "But I was wrong to be suspicious of you before. You were faithful to me. It was my insecurity...but that was then," Ernst said, sheepishly.

"How did you know it was Xavier?"

"I asked Lily if you had been out with anyone else, she said 'yes' and that he was in the South of France. It didn't take a lot of working out. His dream was always the

South of France, the apartment and the Sunseeker. Am I right?"

"Yes," Sienna replied falteringly. "But I want you to know that Xavier and I were never lovers because... because of you..."

He leaned across to her on the sofa, took her in his arms and kissed her passionately, stroking her forehead as he said, "Sienna, I have never loved anyone the way I love you."

She believed him. Sienna beamed and, grasping his hand, replied that she had felt exactly the same and that her feelings for him were still as deep as they'd always been. Nothing had changed.

The next twenty-four hours were a blur of happiness as they renewed their relationship and tender love-making. Ernst brought in Sienna's overnight bag and planted it firmly in the pretty, welcoming spare bedroom from which they hardly moved except to eat and drink. Ernst was happy. The only time he showed a glimpse of deep sadness was when they went to his mother's kitchen to prepare food. The rows of carefully prepared potions and herbal medicines moved him to tears. Sienna mopped his tears and kissed his cheeks, lovingly; it was all she could do.

"I feel so helpless, Ernst."

"Sienna, *Chérie*, having you here is all I need. Just stay with me and never leave. I promise I will never leave you again. Please, please forgive me."

"Nothing to forgive now, Ernst. You were a bit of a mess emotionally! You took a break and it's all sorted now," she replied reassuringly.

"So where do we go from here, Sienna? I have to get back to Corsica as I didn't resign, and I need to pick up my things I left there. I will need to get back and find a job here... but until then, we will be apart, unless you come out to Corsica for a holiday before I return?" He stroked her hand gently, tracing her fingers with the tips of his. "My apartment and the shop has just sold, so I will move into *Maman's* cottage temporarily, as there's plenty to sort out here and decisions to be made." Ernst produced an envelope from his pocket. "I've something to show you, Sienna. I have an envelope and presumably a letter from *Maman*. She left it with the neighbour in case she didn't see me again, but I haven't opened it yet. Whatever was I thinking? I left you and I left my mother too. Look what's happened! I argued with my father and never saw him again."

He put his head in his hands and the tears suddenly flowed. The happy mood had changed, and he was in self-rebuke. Sienna stroked his arm gently, telling him he wasn't to know what would happen.

"Let's open the envelope together?" she suggested.

"I'm scared, Sienna. She may have been angry and..." Sienna shook her head at him and gestured towards the envelope. Ernst finally opened it and after a long pause he read it out to Sienna.

My dearest son,
This is just to say what a wonderful son you are and always have been. I have loved you since I first set eyes on you and nothing has changed. Ernst, whatever you choose to do with your life, you have my blessing. I know you will be successful. Most of all I want you to be happy. I hope you find someone to spend the rest of your life with, whether that be Sienna or not. If it is, which I think it may well be, know that you have my blessing. She's a lovely girl. If it isn't, choose wisely my son. Follow that deep intuition you have and always be true to yourself. Don't lose that wonderful generosity of spirit.
Your father loved you so much, and you gave him much happiness over the years: please recognise that. You have nothing to feel guilty about. Angry words mean nothing. The fire was nothing to do with you. You have always been a wonderful and loving son – have no regrets. We both love you. Treasure our time together, son, but please move on.
From your loving mother, who is smiling down on you. xx

Ernst cried as she'd never seen a man cry. When it reduced to a silent sob, he carefully folded the letter and took it to the old bureau. The tears, however, were of relief, mainly, mixed with the sorrow of his loss. She had known she might die but said nothing!

"See what she said about you, Sienna!"

"I liked her very much," replied Sienna. "A very warm and interesting lady."

"Sienna, I do want to spend the rest of my life with you. I really do. Let me sell the cottage, the sale of the shop is going through and I intend to get a job. Then..." he spoke tentatively, "...we could move in together somewhere? Presuming you're not going back home to England." He hugged her tightly as she nodded and beamed with happiness and felt awash with emotion herself.

"Well, I'm not going anywhere. I'm not leaving Paris," she smiled.

"Right," Ernst pulled himself up and took a manly stance. "I'm going to go straight back to Corsica to collect my things. It will only take a couple of days, then I will come back here and move in until the cottage is sold. We can start gradually looking for somewhere to live? I presume you'd like to live in Saint Germain, in the Latin Quarter?"

Inside, Sienna was astir with excitement. It was the beginning of a new chapter. They celebrated in each other's arms until dark when Ernst put lamps on, poured a drink for them and they listened to music and chatted. They had a lot to catch up on!

Chapter Forty-Two

A beam of strong sunlight shone through the gap in the heavy brocade curtains and lit up a corner of the room. Sienna stretched and opened her eyes, not remembering where she was and thinking she might go to the pool today. There was a deep rhythmic breathing beside her as she turned and saw Ernst fast asleep and looking relaxed. In a second, she remembered... and shot out of bed to run and make coffee. Ernst stirred and wandered to the kitchen looking tousled but happy. They had breakfast and he insisted on booking a flight to Corsica straightaway. Within hours he was packed and ready to go. Sienna took him to the airport and then drove home happily. She ran to the phone, of course, to tell Lily her news. Lily was overjoyed for her, but not really surprised. They agreed to meet up at the Jazz session at the end of the week, when Ernst had returned.
The days passed too slowly for Sienna's liking. She'd missed him as soon as his plane left the runway.

Finally, the day came for his flight to return to Paris. That evening, they headed for the Jazz Club. They wandered again along the dimly-lit street together towards the Club. It reminded her of the first time she had gone there with Xavier. They knocked on the door, but this time they were greeted by Freya, who gave them a drink and ushered them in. It looked different, somehow, though everything was still there. The rustic chairs, worn sofas and tumbling greenery were all in place but there was no-one around.

"Have a seat," Freya said. They sat up and looked up at the wall in front of them. Sienna squealed with delight. The pictures in the middle had been replaced with three of her paintings! Alphonse had had her best character studies framed in dark wood and they made a stunning display. As she turned with her hands over her mouth in sheer surprise there was a commotion from behind the bar and their friends popped out from their hiding places, bearing drinks.

"Surprise!" they cried. "Here's to you two! At last, eh? Welcome home Ernst!" Alphonse lifted his glass. Ernst looked in shock, Sienna giggled like a schoolgirl. A couple of clarinet players in smart navy trousers and wine-coloured waistcoats over white cheesecloth shirts took the floor. The music was bewitching as ever as Ernst and Sienna moved between their delighted friends. The call of "Ernst!" was heard above the music, as everyone welcomed him back. He grinned and savoured his new-found attention, wandering around with Sienna happily in tow. Lily and Emile danced the night away together after greeting them both. Mireille and Michel, looking extremely tanned, welcomed them back, whilst a rather laid-back Theo sat in the corner with his new partner Claude, who, by all accounts, had left the South of France and moved in with Theo already. Sienna caught a glimpse of turquoise frills amidst the revellers and thought it looked like Freya and she was, indeed correct – Freya was draped on Xavier's arm.

"What are you doing here?" Sienna asked in amazement.

"Back here to find an apartment– for us both." It was delightful news – two of Sienna's favourite people together. Alphonse strolled around on his own and spent a long time in conversation with Ernst, looking happy. Sienna secretly hoped that Jean-Luc wouldn't appear. He didn't. He was apparently working in the Maldives. Marie-France and Serge couldn't make it to Paris either and were no longer together.

Alphonse approached Sienna at the end of the evening.

"You rascal," she said. "Pinching my paintings and putting them up here!"

"Oh..." he replied casually. "I'm afraid they won't be here for long, Sienna." She looked at him quizzically. "Afraid so," he said, nodding. "I've sold them for you, at a high price – so you can buy me a drink, eh?!" He laughed.

Sienna blinked as she woke up in her flat the next morning, Ernst beside her again.

"Ernst! Ernst! I do believe I've become an artist! People are really buying my work..."

"Well done, you deserve it! You have a great talent you know," he said, kissing her lips. "Now, I must dash. I've got to don a suit – it will be so hot in this weather – but I have an interview with a magazine on the other side of the city..." Ernst had wanted to pursue a career in journalism and desperately wanted the job. Sienna watched him dress quickly and rush out of the door, wearing a well-cut, linen suit and leaving the aroma of his trademark aftershave as he waved goodbye.

"Sienna Stevenson. Artist," she said out loud. "Oh no, that's all too much..." She decided there and then to remain the way she had signed her paintings. *Sienna S* – it had a better ring.

The phone rang, as it frequently did in Sienna's flat. A man with a deep voice wanted to speak to a certain *Sienna S*: the artist. He had called to commission a painting of his son who was leaving for the army shortly – he wanted it done soon, so would she be able to fit him in? He lived in a rather large old mansion not far from the Etoile and could send his chauffeur to fetch her. He asked her when it would be convenient and told her money would be no object. Sienna arranged a time the day afterwards, pinching herself to ascertain that she wasn't dreaming. *In fact – had she been indeed dreaming all of the happenings of the last few days and weeks?* Ernst arrived home later that afternoon, looking full of beans.

"Got the job!" he declared. "Starting in the near future… can life get any better?" he asked, smiling.

The twists and turns seemed quite incredible as they found time to look for a new home and espied a lovely three-storey old house full of character in the Latin Quarter. It was right near the Jardin Du Luxembourg, which they both loved. Ernst had just sold the shop and apartments and the cottage was on the market too, so they were able to make an offer for the charming old timbered building. Madame LaFargue had left a considerable sum of money too with which Ernst could pay off his debts. They sat on the pavement outside it in the sunshine, making plans, when they were approached by an older gentleman who asked if they happened to know where Theo's shop was.

"Ah, that's easy," Sienna said, pointing him in the right direction. They had agreed to meet Theo for lunch and were surprised when he arrived with the mysterious stranger they'd met earlier.

"Let me introduce Monsieur Vermont," Theo said. "He was directed to me through a friend because I knew you, Ernst." Ernst looked puzzled. Theo ordered a round of drinks.

"You're looking for me?"

"Indeed," he said as he shook Ernst's hand. "I have something to tell you, Ernst. I've been looking for you for a long time, but the last I heard you were abroad. Do you remember the fire a few years back at the Jazz bar?"

"How could I forget?" Ernst replied quizzically.

"Well, I was there. I escaped the fire, but nobody knew. I had a mistress at the time, who sadly died there. I did not want my wife to know. One day, I woke up and knew I had to find you. By then, my wife had left me, so I felt free to say I was there. You see, Ernst, I was with your father just before he died. Your mother had been taken to the ambulance. I tried to revive him, but it was impossible. However, before he died he held my hand and whispered into my ear 'please find my son, Ernst LaFargue. Tell him all is forgiven, and I love him' and with that he passed...it was peaceful at the end, though, Ernst," Monsieur Vermont said with a sigh.

Chapter Forty-Three

Ernst went home with Sienna feeling in a daze of unreality. He felt he needed to pinch himself as everything seemed surreal. They sat and talked quietly about what had happened, Sienna feeling very moved by what just transpired. Ernst felt as though a huge burden had been lifted from his shoulders. He could finally be free of his guilt, his anxiety and his regret. This time it was complete.

"Sienna, I don't think I've ever felt like this," he said, as a solitary tear rolled down his cheek. "Now I am free to enjoy our life and be really happy..."
Sienna held his hand and put her head on his shoulder, knowing what a special day it was for Ernst – and for them.

"Ernst, you need to keep your energy for your new job. Why don't you spend some time with me, looking for things for our new home? It seems it won't be long before it's actually ours now."
Fortunately, the new job was now starting in a month's time and Ernst had time on his hands to think about their future. The house was empty and as soon as they had the keys they could begin deciding how they would furnish it.

"The weather's good so you can go out and about in the sunshine to keep the dreaded asthma at bay, hopefully," Sienna encouraged.

"Is there anything we could use from *Maman's* cottage?" asked Ernst. "I have to empty it this week."

"I'm sure we could Ernst, if you are okay with that. She was a woman of great taste." Sienna's little flat was a good base for them both, temporarily, but already it didn't feel like home to her. She couldn't wait for the keys to their new house: their home. "Now, I have some sketches to deliver to Alphonse and a bit of shopping to do. What are you going to do, my love?"

"I think I will wander around in the sunshine a bit and call in at the *Closerie des Lilas* where I can sit and read for a while."

They set off in opposite directions and Ernst grabbed his book and sunglasses and headed for the café. The waiters greeted him as he had popped in from time to time. The usual old soldiers were still around – sharing stories and drinking coffee. Ernst liked the atmosphere. The camaraderie was good and there was an uplifting spirit of laughter as they told jokes and listened to one of their crowd who was clearly an amusing raconteur. Another round of coffee was ordered, only this time there was also *un bon Cognac.* Ernst looked up from his book and noticed that one of the older men seemed to be staring at him. He wasn't someone that Ernst had seen there before, and he didn't recognise him, although he seemed to be joining in with the general banter. A waiter approached Ernst's table with a rather expensive glass of Cognac that had been sent over by the gentleman on the table opposite. Ernst felt a little puzzled when he waved at him and felt he should go over to thank him and find out what was going on. Most of the others were leaving now and he invited Ernst to take a seat and drink with him. The old man smiled, displaying a full set of even teeth, but his face was weathered and had a 'lived-in appearance'. He looked a little weary as though he had had an eventful life. He spoke hesitantly, with a slight accent which was barely discernible and not familiar to Ernst.

"Please forgive me for intruding and sending you a drink, but I am old now and somewhat lonely. I lost contact with my son many years ago and there was something about you that reminded me of him. My daughter died a few years ago of cancer and I lost my wife last year. I'm sorry to intrude."

"I'm so sorry to hear that," replied Ernst, sensing that the man wanted a bit of company. He introduced himself as Henri and Ernst shook his hand, telling him his name.

"Since my wife died I find myself totally lost in his huge and often impersonal city. Don't misunderstand me – I love Paris. We came here from Switzerland and as we had no family, we bought a small house in the Marais region. My wife loved Paris and she wrote poetry about it, some of which I intend to get published. You cannot beat the romance, the style and the ambiance, can you? Now, what about you?"

Ernst explained a little about his life and talked proudly of Sienna.

"Well, she sounds like a lovely and very talented young lady. Look after her, Ernst. My wife took my daughter's death badly and she never really recovered. My son... well, we are not in contact. Families, eh? You can only really choose your friends, sadly. Please bring your lovely Sienna here. I would be interested to talk about her work. I love Art, you see."

"In that case," said Ernst, warming to him, "why don't you come over to see us? We are at Sienna's apartment but will be moving on to our very own home soon. You could see some of her paintings."

"Oh, that would be wonderful!" Henri replied, his dull eyes acquiring a twinkle. "Here, Ernst, this is my card. Do ring me – I'm genuinely interested. I have a small collection of art but I'm always open to purchasing a few more if something takes my fancy."

The two men shook hands. Ernst stood watching as Henri walked away unsteadily in the direction of the Métro, leaning heavily on his patterned walking cane.

Ernst went back home and told Sienna of the meeting.

"I will ring him next week," said Ernst. "I can't promise that he will buy any of your paintings, Sienna, although he's keen to see them. You will like him though, and I feel somewhat sorry for him – he's so alone here in Paris."

"Ah yes," sighed Sienna sympathetically. "I can identify with that. It's a big city and you can feel very lost and unloved. I'm glad he goes to the *Lilas*. Yes, ask him over for tea – or a meal if you wish. I'm just finishing off a portrait of an English lady at the turn of the century. Maybe that will appeal to him! Although you say he's Swiss – he may not have any connection to or interest in England. Shall we get on with packing a few things up?

Time goes so quickly and before we know it we'll be moving. I understand that we'll be given a date this week." Sienna took a seat as she pondered. "I've been thinking…I'd love a big old oak table and chairs. What do you think?"

"Well, I have so many connections because of the shop we will find one easily. Why don't we get Freya involved with all the bits and pieces?"

"Brilliant idea! I will speak to her later." Sienna beamed.

Chapter Forty-Four

"Hi Freya, it's Sienna."

"Oh, Sienna, hello!" came the reply as she picked up the phone. "How lovely to hear from you. When do you move?" She paused as Sienna updated her. "It's often a bit stressful but it will be a wonderful move for you both. You'd like some help? Of course, I'd be delighted. I'm never happier than choosing and arranging things in a house! You haven't seen our apartment yet – would you and Ernst like to come over for dinner at the weekend? Xavier will be so pleased if you come. You will? Great, that's arranged then. Next Saturday – we'll ring you with the time later. Xavier and I were going to Jazz Club but it's so much better to see you two again!"

Saturday arrived quickly, and they drove over to the new apartment where Freya welcomed them with a hug and ushered them through a light, spacious and airy room. It had obviously been meticulously designed and decorated by Freya, with impeccable attention to detail. It felt almost like walking into a room from a glossy magazine, so well was everything styled. Sienna was a little in awe of Freya's gift and just uttered "Stunning, as always!"

Xavier beamed as they came in and had clearly had his say in the décor. It wasn't a typical Freya-style home. It was white–*very* white: it felt very minimal and contemporary. Sienna knew that look appealed to Xavier. There was white paint, white furniture and white luxurious rugs nestled here and there on the pale wooden floor, the colour of light grey driftwood. Thy sat down at the large rectangular glass table, after having an aperitif on the balcony, which looked out over the rooftops of Paris. The panoramic view was spectacular. Freya had made a great effort to produce her take on a typical English meal and produced roast chicken and vegetables in a gravy. This was accompanied by a wine from Alsace and followed by ice-cream and strawberries. The conversation was lively as they caught up with the latest happenings.

"Did you know that Lily is engaged to Emile now?" Xavier asked. "It's wonderful to see her really happy again..."

"There's been talk of selling the Jazz Club!" Freya informed them.

"Oh no!" cried Sienna. "It's part of us. We must stop this happening!"

They continued with the usual banter and conversation about what was on in Paris – the latest films, shows, must-visit places and restaurants.

"Have you two sorted out any furniture yet?" enquired Xavier.

"No, I need help from Freya!" came the reply as Sienna looked around. Two white, long – but comfortable-looking – sofas faced each other and between them sat soft, furry, white rugs. They housed several arranged cushions, in different textured white fabrics, with delicate abstract patterns. "I do hope you two are not intending to have a family with all this white around!" Sienna laughed.

"Ah. Well, actually..." faltered Freya. "That's one of the reasons we wanted to see you. I'm pregnant!"

"Fabulous!" said Ernst. "I'm sure Xavier is earning enough to replace all the white furnishings!"

"We'd already decorated and never dreamed this would happen," said Freya.

"You're going to make a fabulous mum," Sienna stated. She remembered all the children who used to trail behind Freya. Xavier produced a bottle of *Veuve–Clicquot* rosé champagne – and they drank to the coming event. The laughter and chat continued until Ernst seemed to fall silent. He thought they should summon a taxi and go home.

"But the night is young!" said Freya. "You can stay over here, if you'd like to." Ernst began to breathe quickly, gasping for breath. Sienna rushed to get his inhaler.

"What's the matter darling? It's so rare for you to have an attack. Has something happened that I don't know about?"

"No, no..." protested Ernst. Sienna knew otherwise. A cab was called, and they arrived home quite soon with Ernst breathing better but looking pallid.

"Go and lie down, Ernst," Sienna said, helping him to the bed. His breathing returned to normal eventually and he gave a weak smile as he drank some bottled water.

"Ernst," Sienna said firmly. "Is there anything you need to tell me?"

"Well, yes, I guess so," replied Ernst. "Something strange has happened. Remember Henri, the chap I met at the *Lilas*? Well I rang to invite him over."

"Yes – that's good. He wanted to see my paintings."

"Ah, yes, but I rang him, and he asked if he could see me alone again first, so I stopped by yesterday at the *Lilas*, later in the day."

"I thought you took a while to get back. What happened?"

"I'm so tired now, Sienna. Let's talk in the morning?" Ernst pleaded. The lamp was switched off, the curtains pulled together and as Sienna cuddled up to Ernst, the wine had its heady effect and they slept soundly.

Chapter Forty-Five

The next day was sunny and optimistic-looking with the rays of strong sunshine filtering through the half-open curtains and dancing across their bed, where Sienna held Ernst tightly.

"Let's lie here for a bit and you can tell me what happened with Henri – *oui*?"

"Well..." Ernst said, hesitantly. "I met Henri at the *Lilas* for a drink and chat. He seemed such an amiable man. We got talking about this and that and he said he was a keen gardener and missed his garden a great deal. I told him I loved gardens and plants too." He lowered his eyes. "He told me he knew my mother loved gardens. So, I said to him 'but you didn't know her, Henri!' in surprise to which he responded 'Oh I did, Ernst. Hélène was a wonderful woman and I loved her dearly. We had a son together Ernst...' and looked me in the eye. I said 'No! NO! I can see where this is leading. You are a liar!'"

Ernst took Sienna's hand. "Henri replied that he'd seen an obituary for her and realised who it was. Milly-La-Forêt was mentioned, so he knew she had died. He was at the funeral. Sienna, *he told me I was his son*. I was in a state of shock and I was furious. I said to him 'How dare you! Who are you? You must be a chancer who thinks he can cash in on my inheritance or something. She's never talked about you, and was happily married to my father, Pascal'." He sighed. "He said 'I know this is a shock. I know it's hard. It's really tough for me too.' So, I told him 'Look, Henri – or whatever your name is! I won't listen to this nonsense anymore! I don't believe you even knew my mother. You've seen an obituary and gleaned information about her by visiting Milly'. I told him he could at least honour the dead! After that he stood up, apologised for the upset and said there was no easy way of telling me, but that I should look in the mirror because I have his eyes! He said he knew it the minute he saw me. He told me I have his phone number should I change my mind. I stormed off and practically ran home. I vowed to not let it spoil the weekend: you were so looking forward to seeing Freya and Xavier." Ernst had learned how to control his emotions better when he was in Corsica and he vowed not to cause Sienna any more trouble. Deep down he feared that another trauma might be too much, and she might leave. He finished telling Sienna the tale and saw the tears in her eyes as she held him tight.

"This is awful, Ernst. However, our love is stronger now and we are in this together. I'm here and I'm not going anywhere. We will get through it, my darling," Sienna whispered gently.

"He's an opportunist, Sienna! Scum!"

"Look, Ernst, you have to calm down or your asthma will return. Let's get dressed and go for a walk, eh?" They both dressed and Sienna went to the kitchen to fetch a bottle of water. She heard a bang – it was Ernst slamming the front door as he left. Sienna began to feel very uneasy. She picked up the phone and a voice said calmly, "Yes, Sienna, you may come over now!" It was dear Alphonse inviting her around to his home again. He was such a wise man and dear friend, so she turned to him automatically.

Alphonse welcomed her with open arms and asked her what she would like to eat and drink.

"Nothing, Alphonse, but thank you," she replied. "I just need to tell you something..." She recounted all the latest happenings to him as he shook his head in dismay. "Where Ernst has gone now I really don't know, Alphonse!"

"Dear Sienna, don't worry. Ernst has learnt a great deal about himself of late. He will be back. He may even be home already." Sienna began to sob.

"It's not fair. We were just beginning to see things really settling. Ernst has a new job, and we are moving."

"Life isn't fair, Sienna, my dear. It has its twists and turns and sometimes the unexpected knocks us for six – but we recover, in time, and we are ready for the next round!" Alphonse said wisely. He looked down for a while, pausing before he continued. "To be honest, Sienna, there isn't an awful lot you can do, except to love and support him. He will calm down eventually: you know his temperament. You could agree with him and his suspicions that this man is dishonest – an opportunist – and both agree to cut him out of your lives or...I guess you could go and see him yourself, without telling Ernst and find out the truth? However, if it is true – Ernst is going to be full of anger and not happy that you meddled.

"Oh no!" sighed Sienna. "Do you think it could be true?"

Alphonse paused again.

"I have no idea, Sienna, but I suppose it is a possibility. We all know Ernst's father disappeared when his mother was pregnant. What we don't know is why he left. That's a mystery, as is his identity. Poor Ernst. The intrigue in his life has certainly taken a toll on him from time to time. He's a lovely fellow and I'm so fond of you both."

Sienna fell silent. She got up and admired the artist's latest paintings and sketches. He really seemed to be doing very well for himself nowadays. She admired yet again the strength Alphonse had shown after losing his parents in the fire. She loved his gentle, knowing outlook on life.

"Alphonse, dear Alphonse, thank you. I must go back now to see if Ernst has returned – I will consider what you said." She hugged him tightly and kissed him on the cheek. He smiled sadly as she left him. When she returned Ernst was there at the flat, lying on the sofa, looking rather dazed.

"Where have you been Ernst? I popped out to see Alphonse."

There was no reply, so she went to the kitchen to get some water. She was confronted by a large box in the corner – stacked full of wine. *Strange,* she thought, *I didn't think we were in party mode.* As she went back to Ernst, she realised the truth. An empty wine bottle lay at the end of the sofa and another was in place ready to be drunk. Ernst had stocked up on alcohol to blot out his feelings.

"Oh no, my love," she said tenderly, kissing him on the cheek, as he looked up blearily. "This is not the way we are going to tackle this. You must eat something if you can and drink lots of water. Come on, let's tuck you up next door!"

Ernst staggered to the bedroom and lay on the bed as Sienna fetched him water. He began to cry. He shook with anger and fear as she held him tight. They lay together there in each other's arms until the sun went down and the moon shone a bluish light across the room. Sienna pulled the curtains across and kissed Ernst goodnight.

Chapter Forty-Six

A new day arrived; what it would bring was not clear. Sienna went out to the local shops and returned to find Ernst dressed and sipping coffee calmly. He clearly wasn't happy, but his quick temper had abated, and he sat slowly drinking and just staring at the table with a look of disbelief on his face. Sienna decided she could now reason with him.

"Look, Ernst, we are getting the keys to our new home very soon. Are we going to let this spoil everything we've longed for? A home of our own and a future together?"

"No, no, Sienna, of course not!" replied Ernst. "But how do I move on from this?"

"Well, we either put it behind us – and I mean for good – or we can consider a confrontation with Henri. We could go together, if you wished."

"Not sure if I ever want to see that fellow again, Sienna. Look even if it was true – and I'm sure it isn't – my father walked out on us, before I was even born; he didn't want me. He rejected me and he hurt my dear mother. Pascal was my dad, and he always will be."

"Yes, I understand that," Sienna sympathised. "It's a lot to take in. Shall we discuss it again later?"

"No, Sienna. I feel like a dog with a bone. It won't go away. I think you should ring the man and we will meet him together and confront him."

"Are you sure, Ernst?"

"I can't promise to be polite or not get angry, but yes we must put the whole sorry saga to bed."

"If you think you might get angry we'd better not meet in a public place, Ernst?"

"I need the freedom of being able to walk away. If he comes here, it could be awkward to be rid of him."

"I'll ring him this evening then if you give me his card." Luckily Ernst hadn't ripped it up in anger.

Henri was surprised to receive a phone call from Sienna, asking if the three of them could meet. They eventually decided to meet at a small café off the beaten track in a quiet side street where there would be no prying eyes. Ernst was happy with that. Well, not quite *happy*, but resigned. The following day they met up and ordered drinks to make them feel as mellow as possible in this awkward tête-á-tête. Henri spoke first, quietly and calmly.

"Look, I know this is a dreadful shock to both of you – you in particular, Ernst." Ernst sat with pursed lips and an unfriendly expression on his face. "Please hear me out," pleaded Henri. "I am an honest man and I have no ulterior motive. I met your mother when we were very young. She was a wonderful, warm, beautiful lady. We were very much in love. We did not marry although we were together several years as Hélène had problems with her parents. She never stopped caring for their every need. They were both quite ill with different complaints and her father had MS and was confined to a wheelchair. She lived with them and was so incredibly unselfish. Does that ring a bell, Ernst?"

Ernst had turned incredibly pale but said, "Yes, that's all very true but you could have easily gotten that information. How do I know it's genuine?"

Henri continued, as Sienna took Ernst's hand. "I started to feel unwell about the time she became pregnant. It wasn't planned but we were both thrilled. I had lots of tests and was eventually diagnosed with MS – I couldn't tell your mother. She devoted her life to looking after her father in a wheelchair and had a sick mother. I loved her so dearly – I couldn't ruin her life and present her with someone else to care for, so I left; it almost killed me." A tear trickled down his cheek. "I left the woman I loved to bring up our child into a carefree environment. She never knew – but I softened the blow as much as I could by leaving her a considerable amount of money, telling her how much I would always love her and the child, but it was for the best. Sadly, for us both, my MS was misdiagnosed and two years later I was clear of a very

191

debilitating and rare illness. I cried myself to sleep for so many nights, but I know I did it for you and your mother. Can you forgive me at all?"

He looked over at Ernst, who was even paler, and his eyes had misted over. Sienna held his hand tightly and choked on her tears. The emotion of the moment was overpowering. Eventually, Henri said, "Ernst, my son, look in the mirror when you get home. I stared at you in the *Lilas* because you are the image of your mother – I'm sure you have been told that many times. However, you have my eyes"

There was nothing more to be said. Henri got up and paid the bill. He went over to Ernst and offered him his hand.

"Will you shake my hand, son, and let me into your life? I've dreamed of this moment for so long..."

Ernst felt a hopeless mess of emotions. He held out a shaky hand to Henri and then the two men embraced and Henri kissed Sienna on the cheek. "I'm going home now; I'm an old man and tired. If you could find it in your heart to keep in touch, I would be honoured, Ernst. There's so much to talk about – so many years to catch up on..."

Ernst stifled a sob and grasped Sienna's hand as they made their way home, almost in silence and overcome by the emotion of the moment.

"Looks like you have a dad, Ernst!" Sienna said brightly, at last.

"Yes," replied Ernst. There was a silence. "I've got what I always wanted – to know my real dad. I hope I can handle it, Sienna. It's a terrific shock."

Chapter Forty-Seven

The next day was again bright and sunny. The mood chez Sienna was equally light. Ernst had tossed and turned all night, whilst Sienna slept. He didn't feel tired, though, despite the poor sleep. Sienna fetched him a coffee on waking. His very first words to her were "Sienna, I have a dad! I'm going to have a dad again! I will never forget my father who brought me up, though. Pascal was a wonderful man..."

"You don't have to," replied Sienna. "But let's enjoy some time with Henri whilst he's still around. That was an amazing thing he did, you know."

"It was," Ernst said. "To think I've always hated my dad for leaving us and I thought it was my fault because he didn't want me."

"It seems that couldn't be further from the truth!" Sienna exclaimed. "Look, he's lonely. He's had no one to love or love him for a while, but now he has us. Let's get in touch and ask him over." Suddenly, the phone rang, and Ernst answered. A gentleman was calling to announce they could pick up the keys to their new house today!

"Oh wow!" said Sienna. "Let's go get them and go to the house! Then we can gradually move furniture in over the next week or so when I give up the flat."

"Great! Great!" said a voice. The parrot was joining in with the celebrations and it made them laugh.

"I'm afraid you've gotta go soon, stupid bird," Ernst told him rather sternly.

"Right, let's go then! I want those keys!" Sienna said. They strolled off into the sunshine, Sienna noting that Ernst had the hint of a smile on his face.

"Let's go somewhere and have lunch to celebrate," Ernst suggested.

"Why don't we ask Lily and Emile if they'd like to come?"

"No," replied Ernst. "I'm not ready to tell anyone yet. Let's go and celebrate quietly. We are about to enter a new phase of our lives with a new house and another member of the family, it seems."

"I'm just getting a bit excited about everything!" Sienna laughed. "How do you feel?"

"I'm really excited about the house, of course. The situation with Henri – er, *my father* – is gradually sinking in. I'm so glad he had a reason to leave Maman, sad though the story is. It will take time to adjust, I guess, but I already feel a warmth for him. Let's have lunch, then go on to our new home."

Lunch was outside at a quiet bistro they knew well. Neither of them was especially hungry so had a snack with a glass of wine and then hurried off to the house. It was, of course, near the Jardin du Luxembourg, so they strolled through and eventually arrived at the house. The shutters were closed and then road was quite deserted. They turned the key and entered the interesting-looking building. It was empty, of course, but as they walked in they immediately sensed a warmth of atmosphere. It was a feeling you get when you instantly like someone's house. A kind of aura – a *je ne sais quoi* – exuded everywhere. It was small but cosy. The old hearth in the sitting room leant character to the room along with the stripped pine beams and warm-coloured tiled floor. The kitchen was completely empty but overlooked a small courtyard where the last owner had left quite a few old pots. Sienna eyed them with excitement, knowing that the following year they could be full of colour.

"We will need to make it a priority to re-furbish the kitchen," Ernst said. "But we still have your place for a few weeks more. I think I need to go over to Milly. *Maman's* furniture is still there temporarily and there are several pieces we want."

"Not much, though, Ernst, I'd like to start again. Is that OK?"

"Of course, Sienna, we will make it *ours*. I think you wanted the pretty old standard lamp?"

"Oh, yes, I love that. But, really, that's all. Is there anything you want, Ernst?"

"No – too many memories that I would prefer to let go of, except, of course, when I choose to think about *Maman*."

"Are you sure, darling?"

"Well, I guess the bedside tables would be good to have and maybe her garden chair would be nice in the courtyard..."

"That's fine. Xavier says you can borrow a little van that a friend of his drives."

The steps up to the bedrooms and bathroom were steep and creaked as they went up excitedly. There were three roomy bedrooms: two on the first floor and one in the spacious attic. Light streamed in through the long, horizontal window of the attic room.

"May I..." Sienna began.

"...have this as my art studio?" Ernst finished for her.

"I've always wanted an atelier of my own." Sienna beamed.

"Of course, *Chérie*. I know it would be perfect for you."

Back in the flat after a long day of planning what to buy and where to go, Ernst decided to go to Milly the next day, whilst Sienna would order a sofa and chairs they had seen.

"Shall I ring Henri?" Sienna asked. "Perhaps he would like to come here tomorrow evening and look at my paintings."

Ernst paused, then, rather misty-eyed, agreed it would be a good idea.

Chapter Forty-Eight

Henri arrived exactly on time. He had an old car which he only used for trips around the city nowadays. Sienna welcomed him with a kiss on the cheek and ushered him in, smiling broadly.
"*Bienvenue, Henri!*" she said, grasping his hand and guiding him into the lounge. Then, the unexpected happened. Henri walked rather falteringly and nervously into the lounge, where Ernst stood rather anxiously too.
"Ernst... my son..." he said.
"Dad!" said Ernst, in tears, as they hugged each other so tightly you would never have dreamed they could ever let go of the embrace. Henri was overcome with emotion. Sienna tactfully went into the kitchen to make drinks, feeling quite overcome herself by the sight of the two men finding each other after all those years. She took the drinks in on a tray, with a box of tissues for them all.
"This is unbelievable," Henri finally said. "God has been merciful. I never thought I would have a family again. Thank you both so much for hearing me out and accepting me." None of them were hungry so Sienna brought out various snacks and delicacies and decided to freeze the *Coq au Vin* she had made.
"Henri," she said, taking a seat. "Tell us more about your life. Were you born in Switzerland?"
"Yes, I was," replied Henri. "My parents were German though and my father was called Ernst. Hélène always liked the name, you see. I had a happy childhood there. The air was so fresh and the people all so friendly. I loved it there – but I met a French lady when I was quite young: your mother, Ernst. She was so beautiful, lively and intelligent that I fell instantly in love with her. Her eyes danced with merriment when she was happy, and sometimes they would shine. She had the same attractive, lustrous hair you have too. She was quite quietly spoken, like you."
Ernst smiled.

"What was she doing in Switzerland? Or did you meet in France?" he asked.

"Yes, we met in Switzerland. She was there staying with friends. She had brought her parents from Paris to see if the clear Swiss air might help them both feel better. I have photos of my parents and us, which I will find and show you next time."

"That would be amazing!" Sienna said with enthusiasm.

"Hélène wanted me to go back to Paris with her and I was in agreement but didn't know if I would find work. I had grown up 'around wood' you see. My father had been a wood turner and I loved the feel and smell of wood. I became a cabinet-maker and carpenter, working for a lot of High Society people, helping in their lovely and, sometimes large, houses..."

"That's strange. Well, perhaps not *so* strange!" interjected Ernst. "I love wood too and furniture. I've just sold my little shop where I had high-end antiques for sale. The smell and feel of wood is amazing to me."

It was an interesting conversation that went on all evening, as Ernst told Henri about his life.

"Sienna and I would love you to come to our new house. We are furnishing it at the moment."

"Oh, of course. I shall look forward to it, my dears. As you know, I have plenty of time on my hands. I'm a real handyman and I could make things for you. What do you say?"

"Well," Sienna replied, looking at Ernst who nodded in agreement. "We could do with some kitchen cupboards, pretty urgently."

"No problem. I will meet you there soon then?"
They both grinned at him.

Chapter Forty-Nine

The busy days turned into weeks. Henri had by now ordered all of the required wood and fittings and worked industriously and happily in the kitchen. He only stipulated one thing – that no-one should see it before it was finished! He protested at being offered payment, saying it was a *labour of love*. Slowly, their house was coming together. The sitting room was already extremely cosy, with logs on the hearth, ready for Autumn, a comfortable squishy sofa with masses of soft cushions and a warmly patterned Persian rug. In one corner stood the beautiful standard lamp from Milly, with its pretty floral shade that Sienna so admired. An oak coffee table and side tables were stacked tidily with magazines and books.

One evening they sat having a drink there and Henri came in, having finished another long day in the kitchen.

"Only a few more things left to do in there and cooking can begin!" he announced proudly. That was a relief as they'd been mainly eating out, as they'd now moved from Sienna's apartment. Henri espied the lamp in the corner.

"Ah...that lamp! I bought it for Hélène all those years ago and she had kept it. I'm very touched by that. My beautiful Hélène!" A single tear dropped down his face, which he quickly wiped away.

"Yes," said Ernst. "It will be a memento of my childhood too. I'm glad we have it!"
Sienna got up to go out, leaving them to talk.

"Where are you off to?" asked Henri.

"I have a delivery to make! We have had this wretched parrot – or *I* have – for too long and I'm so fed up with its bilingual commentary on my life. It's a lovely bird and deserves someone who will love it. I'm taking it to a shop."

"Oh no!" said Henri. "Let me have it. My house is so silent, and it will be company for me."

Sienna smiled gratefully and heaved a sigh of relief.

One day the following week, Henri phoned before he arrived and said excitedly, "Today is the grand opening of your kitchen! So please both be around this afternoon to see it. I shall be there at three o'clock!"

The excitement was unbearable for Sienna. She simply couldn't wait. There was just a little voice inside her that said: *Whatever shall I say if I don't like it?*

"I'm not good at hiding my emotions, Ernst..." she confessed. "Well you know that."

"We will have to pretend and try to live with it," Ernst said firmly. "Look at the time he's spent on it, to say nothing of the fact he's bought everything in it as a gift!"

Three o'clock arrived, and so did Henri, clutching a bottle of fine champagne. He opened the thick oak door and invited them into the kitchen, Sienna going first.

"Oh wow! Oh, my goodness, Henri! What have you done?"

Ernst followed and looked in amazement. All of the units were of dark, solid oak, in a simple style. There was a round sunken light grey sink and exquisite silver taps with unusual grooving on them. The floor was light stone and a neutral-coloured blind had been put up at the window, which overlooked the courtyard. Every appliance they needed blended in immaculately. The thing that stood out the most, however, was to be found in one corner of the room: there was an amazing arrangement of little green bottles in all shapes and sizes. As they neared them and looked more closely, Sienna and Ernst noticed they were all labelled with beautiful handwriting in black ink.

"Look, Ernst!" Sienna cried out. "This one says *Rosemary*, and this is a little bag of *Herbes de Provence*, the jar next to it is *Chamomile*..."

"*Oh la-la, Sienna!* It's just like *Maman's* kitchen!" They were overwhelmed.

"How did you know, Henri? You never went to the cottage. This is incredible!" Ernst said, emotion arising in him yet again.

"No, I never saw the cottage kitchen," replied Henri, "but I knew Hélène very well – even then she was obsessed with herbs and natural medicine. She had her green jars all lined up in the kitchen and began making potions to try and help her parents. She told me then: 'This is for life, Henri, it's going to be my *raison d'être*, my job.' It matters that people have an alternative to often dangerous drugs."

Sienna and Ernst were speechless as they hugged Henri and he popped open the champagne. This man was truly a gem and they were becoming so close to him in such a short time.

"You are an angel in disguise!" Sienna laughed. "We both thank you from the bottom of our hearts."

Henri beamed. "The thanks are mine. I have a family at last, that means more than anything..."

The happy day ended at a little restaurant around the corner where they had invited their friends to meet Henri. Sienna had already told the complex tale to them over the phone. They were all eager to meet him. Theo arrived first and shook Henri's hand. They chatted for a while and seemed to be getting on famously. Then Alphonse, Lily and Emile came, followed by Xavier and Freya. Mireille couldn't come, sadly. The food was ordered along with several bottles of white wine (the best, of course, and bought by Xavier). The conversation was lively as they hadn't been together for a while and there was lots of catching up to do. Alphonse sat next to Henri and they immediately hit it off: a firm friendship was formed that day. Alphonse invited Henri to his home later in the week and the two men chatted as though they had known each other forever. Henri had never felt happier and it showed. Sienna and Ernst laughed and joked as they ate and drank the delicious fare.

As evening drew in slowly, they went their separate ways, with everyone kissing Henri on the cheek and shaking his hand. Ernst walked back, hand in hand with Sienna: he looked a happy man.

"Let me take you to the rooftop restaurant for another drink before we go back?" he said.

"Another drink...? Oh, well, perhaps one more."
They turned off into a side street and Ernst led her up a rather ornate staircase to the garden bar. Here you could sit on the terrace with a drink, surrounded by huge, green, architectural plants and look over the rooftops of Paris for miles beyond.

"Isn't it beautiful, Sienna? Our home – and hopefully our children's, when we are married. We will be married, won't we, Sienna? I sometimes wonder if you might get so homesick you will have to go home to England."

"Ernst!" Sienna said in amazement, cuddling up to him. "We will be married and have lots of wonderful children. As for leaving this place – you must be joking! I was looking at all our friends today, and your father. More has happened to me since I arrived here than I could have ever imagined. It's magical!" She looked out into the distance. "I now truly feel like a Parisienne at last."

Ernst smiled. "There's something about Paris, isn't there?"
This needed no reply.

About the Author

Vivien Lacey

Vivien Lacey was born by the sea in Norfolk. As a young teenager, she joined the twinning of her hometown with Rambouillet near Paris. Her many visits to France and a year in Paris as part of a French degree left her with an insatiable yearning for French life, people and style. In her debut novel, she has drawn on her own experiences to try to convey the true ambiance of the "City of Light". When not writing, Vivien's other passion lies with art.